Heartland™

New Beginnings

Lauren Brooke

■SCHOLASTIC

With special thanks to
Gill Harvey

Scholastic Children's Books,
Euston House, 24 Eversholt Street,
London NW1 1DB, UK
a division of Scholastic Ltd

London ~ New York ~ Toronto ~ Sydney ~ Auckland
Mexico City ~ New Delhi ~ Hong Kong

First published in the UK by Scholastic Ltd, 2004
Series created by Working Partners Ltd

10 digit ISBN 0 439 96401 6
13 digit ISBN 978 0439 96401 2

Printed and bound by Nørhaven Paperback A/S, Denmark

4 6 8 10 9 7 5

Chapter One

"Come on, Red. Come on, Ben! You can do it. Just one more," Amy Fleming muttered to herself, her hands clenched as she willed the horse and rider on to the final fence. The chestnut gelding rose gracefully into the air, tucking his front hooves into his chest, and soared over the top pole with almost a foot to spare.

"Fantastic!" cried Amy, joining in the applause that rippled around the arena.

"That was a clear round for Ben Stillwell on What Luck," announced the commentator.

Amy left her seat and headed for the far end of the showground, knowing Ben would head for his trailer, which was parked there. She was so happy to be at a show for a few hours. Almost a year had passed since she had been on the competition circuit, but Amy felt the familiar adrenaline rush return – despite the fact that she was just there as a spectator for a short spell. Her grandfather, Jack Bartlett, had needed to pick up a part for his tractor nearby, so it had been an ideal opportunity for her to see Ben. Her old friend had been competing at events all over the country, but this showground was the closest to Amy's home and she had jumped at the chance to see him in action. Ben had been a stable hand at Heartland, where Amy lived and worked with troubled horses. Leaving Heartland had been a tough decision for him, but

Amy knew he'd made the right choice. He now had a position at Nick Halliwell's showjumping yard, and the life clearly suited both him and Red, his spirited chestnut. They seemed to be claiming a championship ribbon every week.

On her way to meet up with Ben and Red, Amy passed one of the show's warm-up rings, where five or six horses were cantering in circles and jumping over the practice jumps. She was making a routine pass when one of the horses caught her eye. She stopped and craned her neck to get a closer look.

The muscular grey gelding on the far side of the ring seemed very familiar.

"Mercury!" she whispered.

After a few moments, Amy recognized his rider, too. It was Bruce Haslam, one of the pair of trainers who now owned him. Amy scanned the area for Gabriel Adams, Mercury's co-owner. When she did not see him, she returned her focus to the ring and watched as Bruce pointed the gelding towards the row of jumps. Mercury's ears flickered, then pricked forward as he collected his stride and bounded over the first. The practice jumps were low, and the grey gave a playful buck as he landed safely over the second, then steadied himself to clear the third.

Amy smiled. She knew Mercury well. He was one of the many horses that had come to Heartland for help. Looking at Mercury now, there was no sign of his former problems. Bruce and Gabriel had bought Mercury over a year ago and had soon discovered that his previous owners had rapped his forelegs – a harsh practice of hitting a horse's legs as he goes over a fence to make him jump higher. By the time Mercury was settled at Bruce and Gabriel's yard, the trauma from his intense training had turned him against jumping altogether. He refused to approach even the tiniest obstacle. It had seemed as though Mercury might never compete again – yet here he was, back in his element and loving every minute of it.

As Bruce slowed Mercury to a trot, Amy thought about how she had treated the troubled gelding. It hadn't been conventional, even by Heartland standards. She had failed to reach him through join-up and her mother's herbal remedies. She and Ty, who was Amy's boyfriend as well as Heartland's head stable hand, had argued about whether Mercury still had the competitive spirit. Amy had believed that the horse would regain the spark that he had shown in the show ring as a youngster, but Ty had felt otherwise. It was one of their first differences after they had taken over the day-to-day running of Heartland.

Amy had had faith that Mercury would recover. Having tried the typical Heartland techniques, Amy decided to take Mercury to Ten Beeches – a stable deep in the Appalachian Mountains, near a village called Ocanumba. She went there to get the advice of a Native American horse healer named Huten Whitepath. Huten had been a friend of Amy's mother, and he had shown Amy how to help Mercury rediscover jumping on his own terms. Huten believed Mercury would reclaim his love of jumping once he was able to approach an obstacle willingly and with confidence. He had been right.

On an impulse, Amy jogged over to the ringside and waved

to catch Bruce's attention.

His lean, handsome face broke into a smile. "Hey! Amy! Good to see you," he greeted her, trotting over. "How are you? Are you riding here today?"

Amy shook her head. "No, I just have a few hours off to come and watch Ben." She reached up and patted Mercury's neck. "He's looking great. How's he doing?"

Bruce grinned. "Wonderfully," he said. "Three blue and two red ribbons in the last two months. He's so much happier now. You did a fantastic job with him, Amy. Gabriel still sings your praises every day. And so do I!"

As if in agreement, Mercury snorted.

"I'm glad," said Amy, feeling gratified. Gabriel and Bruce were experienced trainers and their opinion was worth a lot. She smiled as Mercury jangled his bit. "He sure looks like he's raring to go today," she said. "Which class are you in? I'd love to come and watch."

"We'll be in the main ring in about half an hour," said Bruce. "First round of the Open. You might spot Gabriel ringside, too."

"Great, I'll be there. I should find Ben now, before he thinks I've got lost," said Amy, waving. "Good luck!" She hurried along the railed-off walkway to the collecting ring. She could see that Ben had dismounted close to the entrance to the ring and was loosening Red's girth while his friend, Tara, held on to the reins. Red didn't look the least bit tired – his ears were pricked and his whole expression was alert. As long as he didn't get overexcited and wear himself out, Amy knew he stood a good chance of winning his class in the jump-off. There were few horses that could jump as fast as him over a difficult, twisting course.

"Hi!" she greeted Ben and Tara. "Red looked great!"

"Yeah, he's going well," Ben agreed. "I just need to keep him calm before the jump-off."

Tara stroked the gelding's damp neck. "He's pretty fired up," she said. "Maybe we should take him back to the trailer, away from all the action."

Amy smiled to herself. Nick Halliwell's stables had given Ben more than just the showjumping lifestyle he wanted. It was also where he'd met Tara. They had a lot in common and had hit it off right away. Tara kept her beautiful grey cob, Apollo, at the yard, and while she often showed herself, today she had come just to support Ben.

As they walked back towards the Halliwell trailer, Amy's thoughts returned to Mercury, and she realized that Ben would probably remember him. "I've just seen a familiar face," she said. "Mercury, the horse I took down to Ocanumba. Do you remember him?"

"Of course," Ben replied. "If I recall, you had asked me to try working with him before you took him away. I didn't get very far." He frowned at the thought. "Thanks for the good memory, Amy. I think I'm much happier concentrating on Red."

Amy shrugged. "Come on. You know I didn't get very far with him, either, until Huten began to help," she pointed out.

"I guess," said Ben easily. "Well, Ocanumba sounded pretty special. Have you heard from Huten lately?"

5

Amy shook her head as memories of the beautiful Appalachian region came flooding back. With a pang of regret, she thought of Carey, Huten's granddaughter, who was Amy's age. They had become good friends during Amy's visit, but somehow they'd lost contact in recent months.

"I haven't talked to them for a while," she admitted. "Maybe I should give them a call. Huten would love to see Mercury now — he looks fantastic. It's too bad I didn't bring a camera with me. Do you want to come with me to watch him jump? Bruce is riding him in the Open in about twenty minutes."

"I'd love to," said Ben enthusiastically. "Would you mind, Tara?"

"Go ahead. I'll watch Red," said Tara, reaching out to take the reins from Ben.

Amy and Ben left Tara with the chestnut gelding and headed to the main ring, where the Open jumping was well under way. They watched three other horses before Mercury entered the ring, his nostrils flaring, with Bruce only just managing to contain him. As soon as the bell sounded, the pair flew around the jumps, judging each one perfectly. Mercury took to the course with pure exuberance. It was difficult to imagine he had ever lost his interest in competing.

"He's quite a horse," commented Ben as Mercury cantered through the finishing gate after a flawless, clear round.

Amy nodded. "He'll go far. All thanks to Huten," she agreed. She smiled, thinking of the gentle Native American who had known exactly how to read the troubled gelding's mind and understood how to help him discover his love of jumping again.

"Hi, Lou," Amy greeted her sister, pushing open Heartland's kitchen door. "Another triumph for Ben Stillwell and What Luck!"

Lou looked up from the papers she was poring over. "*What Luck?*" Her expression was blank.

"Red's show name," Amy reminded her. "What Luck."

"Oh! Yes. Well, good for him," said Lou. "Did they win their class?"

"Yup," said Amy. "There's no stopping them. I saw an old Heartland horse, too – Mercury. The one I took to Ten Beeches, remember? We saw him in the first round of the Open, and he's jumping his heart out."

Lou stood up and filled the kettle with water. "That must have been a good feeling," she said. "He wasn't an easy horse to figure out. Do you want a cup of coffee?"

"Yes, please," said Amy. She cast her eye over the glossy brochures on the table. "What are these? Catering companies for the wedding?"

Lou ran a hand through her short blonde hair. "Yes. Amy, they're such a rip-off! They all do the same cold cuts and salads, and they charge a fortune. Everything that has anything to do with a wedding seems three times as expensive as it should be."

Amy instantly felt guilty. Lou's wedding budget had been dramatically reduced when she'd used her savings to rescue five horses from a disreputable auction house. After they had arrived at Heartland in an illegal trailer, Lou bought the horses outright to avoid them being transported elsewhere in the inhumane vehicle. The youngest horse, a gangly roan yearling named Spindleberry, had captured Amy's heart from the moment he'd arrived. She had persuaded Lou to let her keep him and, at least for a couple of years, train him using Heartland methods. Thinking of this, Amy felt partly responsible for her sister's limited budget.

All the same, Amy knew that if Lou had to make the decision again, she would do exactly the same thing. The whole episode had been very distressing. Amy's boyfriend, Ty, had received a call from his father, a truck driver. Brad said he was bringing his load to Heartland instead of the auction yard but offered nothing more. When he arrived, they'd made a shocking discovery. After a six-hour drive, all eight horses in the cramped, overheated trailer had been severely traumatized and dehydrated; two of them had already died. Another had been barely able to stand. Scott, the local vet who was also Lou's fiancé, had put the palomino mare down as an act of kindness when it was clear she would not recover.

"Maybe we could sell Libby and Bear, once they're ready to be rehomed," Amy suggested, naming two of the rescued horses. "They'll make very reliable riding horses."

"No, no, no, we can't do that," Lou protested. "We'll give them to good homes along with the other two. You shouldn't feel bad, Amy. It's not only about money. I was just thinking that we'd have much nicer food if we did the catering ourselves, that's all."

Amy's eyes widened. "For a whole wedding?" she gasped. "You can't do that, Lou!"

"What do you mean?" asked Lou indignantly, putting her hands on her hips.

Amy scrutinized her sister. "You're joking," she said. "You are going to be in your white dress, an apron and oven mitts on your big day? Are you crazy?"

Lou grinned. "No, I'm not," she said. "But I do have something up my sleeve – a secret weapon, so to speak." She took in a big breath. "I was thinking of asking Nancy to help. I have a sneaky feeling she might enjoy it. What do you think?"

Amy laughed. Lou was right. Nancy was their grandpa's friend and a wonderful cook. She loved being involved in what was going on at Heartland and, like Lou, she was also highly organized. "Well, I imagine you two could manage anything once you put your heads together," Amy agreed.

Lou looked pleased. "I hope so," she said. "Let's hope Nancy thinks so, too."

After finishing her coffee, Amy headed out into the yard to see what had happened at Heartland in her absence. Down in the bottom training ring, she found Ty riding the grey mare Liberty, one of the five rescued horses. Ty had given her a long rein, allowing her to stretch out her neck at the end of her training session. Amy approached quietly, knowing how nervous the mare could be. Although her broad forehead and straight nose showed that she was generous and good-natured, she was also very sensitive and had been profoundly affected by the terrible experience she had gone through.

Fortunately, at fifteen, Libby still had a future as a steady riding horse, and she was gradually regaining her strength and confidence with careful handling and the use of many herbal remedies. As Amy opened the gate, Ty rode Libby over, and the mare gave a snort of greeting. Amy was glad to see that her soft brown eyes were calm and friendly. She was getting there.

"Hello, Libby," she said, reaching out to stroke her velvety muzzle. She smiled up at Ty. "Good day?"

Ty dismounted and gave Amy a quick kiss. "Pretty good," he said. "How about you?"

Amy filled him in on the excitement of Ben's win, then told him about seeing Mercury. "It was good to see him jumping so well, after all he'd been through," she said. "He's back to his old self now – a real show-off."

"Glad to hear it," said Ty. "Bruce and Gabriel must be happy about that."

Amy nodded. "Bruce said they were both thrilled."

They walked back up to the yard together, passing Joni, the stable girl who had joined them when Ben had left. She was lunging Bear, a thirteen-year-old gelding that had been in the truck with Libby. With his placid, accepting nature, Bear was recovering more quickly than Libby and would soon be ready for a new home. Joni raised the lunge whip in greeting, then turned back to the bay horse.

"I should be able to fit in a quick session with Spindle before the evening feeds," said Amy as Ty unbuckled Libby's girth. "Is he in the top pasture with the others?"

"Yes, I turned him out this morning," answered Ty. "I'm sure he's pining for you."

Amy grinned and headed to the tack room for a lead rope. She loved the challenge of training a young horse, and her bond with Spindleberry was no secret. She jogged down to the pasture, humming to herself, and as the yearling raised his head and whinnied, her heart gave a little leap of happiness.

"Hi, Spindle!" she called.

The gangly youngster trotted over. Of the five horses from the trailer, he had recovered the quickest, mainly because he was young and had been able to bounce back from the physical effects of the heat and dehydration. He had received very little training before arriving at Heartland, but now he was responding willingly to Amy and seemed to enjoy learning new things.

She snapped the lead rope on to his halter and led him to the yard.

"I'm going to show you what a bit is today," she told him. He was far too young to be ridden, but the earlier he accepted pieces of tack, the easier he'd find it when he had to wear them for real. She tied him to one of the metal rings outside the tack room and went inside to get a gentle rubber snaffle. When she came out again, Spindle was nibbling at the metal ring, his ears twitching in curiosity.

"Hey!" laughed Amy. "Why don't you try nibbling this instead?"

She placed the snaffle flat on her hand and allowed the yearling to probe it with his upper lip. She slippèd it into his mouth, and Spindle chewed on it in surprise before letting it drop out of his mouth again.

"Good boy," said Amy, patting him. "Can we try that again?"

This time, Spindle wasn't so sure about the strange new object. He kept his teeth clenched, and Amy had to persuade him to open up again by squeezing gently on the sides of his mouth. When he relented and took the bit once more, Amy rewarded him with a few horse cookies. He chomped exaggeratedly at them, sending sticky white foam spattering over Amy. Laughing, she stepped away. She knew it was a good sign if the bit made him produce extra saliva, because it indicated that he was relaxed about having the unfamiliar object in his mouth.

By the end of the session, Spindleberry was perfectly at ease with the bit, opening his mouth for Amy to slip it up beyond his incisors, and then letting her slide it back out without panicking.

"That'll do," she said. "I don't want you getting bored." She washed the bit and returned it to the tack room, then led Spindle back to the pasture. He was full of curiosity, and Amy allowed him to investigate anything that caught his eye, knowing the exposure to new things now would make him much less nervous later on. Hanging baskets, wheelbarrows, plastic feed bags, the yard hose – Spindle wanted to take a good look at them all, and he wanted to eat most of them, too.

Halfway down the path, Joni appeared, leading Bear to the yard. Spindle greeted the gelding with a high-pitched whinny, and Bear snorted in reply. Amy and Joni stopped to let the pair touch noses.

"Spindle's looking so alert and inquisitive," Joni commented.

"You're doing a great job with him, Amy."

"Oh, thanks," said Amy, her heart warming. "He's a very willing pupil and a fast learner. That helps."

"Adoring his owner helps, too," agreed Joni with a laugh. She gave Bear's lead rope a tug. "Come on, Bear. Time for a rubdown."

As Amy arrived at the pasture, the sun was setting, sending long pink rays across the grass. She unclipped Spindle's halter and watched as he cantered away, shaking his mane. It was a warm summer evening, and he would be fine staying out for the night. Amy smiled as he stopped and turned round to gaze at her. Despite the trauma of the double-decker trailer, Spindle's future was looking bright.

That night was warm and sticky. Amy had trouble sleeping and threw off her cover as she tossed and turned. Eventually, she dozed off, flitting in and out of restless dreams. There were trees all around her, stretching away into the shadows. She was riding through a forest. She had the sense of following someone familiar along a winding track, urging her horse to catch up. On and on they went, the silence of the forest broken only by the creaking of her leather saddle and the snapping of twigs under her horse's feet. At last, after many miles, they reached a clearing by a stream. Amy looked round. The familiar figure stepped forward, and Amy strained to see who it was. She looked and looked, but suddenly there was no one there.

Amy woke with a jump and stared into the darkness, wiping beads of sweat from her forehead. The dream had seemed so vivid, and yet she couldn't quite place it. She struggled to work it out, but the images were fading, and all that remained was a dull sense of sadness. She thought back to the prior evening, trying to think what had triggered the dream. All she could recall was Spindle. At the thought of the yearling, she smiled. With a sigh, she turned over and managed to fall back to sleep.

Amy got up at six as usual. She pulled on her yard jeans and shirt, and headed out into the early morning light. She loved going down to the pastures at this time of day, when the grass glistened with dew and a few wisps of mist still lingered in the air.

Most of the horses were grouped together, dozing. Spindleberry was lying down with two of the rescued horses, Aria and Shalom, but he scrambled to his feet and walked over sleepily when Amy called. She scratched his neck and gave him an apple, glancing casually at the dense woods towards Clairdale Ridge. With a start, her dream from the night before came back to her. Those deep forests – she knew where they were. Of course! They were at Ocanumba. Seeing Mercury at the show must have triggered her memory. *I need to call Huten and Carey*, she thought. *Before I forget.*

After giving Spindle a final pat, she walked back to the yard to start the morning chores. Ty and Joni soon joined her and, with so many horses out for the night, it didn't take long to finish the feeding and mucking out. By seven-thirty, Amy headed back indoors.

After a quick breakfast, she hunted in the office for the

phone number of Ten Beeches, the stables in Ocanumba where Huten lived with his son Bill, Bill's wife Barbara, and of course Carey.

"What are you looking for?" asked Lou, sipping coffee in the doorway.

"I'm looking for Huten's number," Amy confessed. She felt guilty that it was so long since she'd used it. "Seeing Mercury yesterday made me think I should give him a call."

"It's a good thing you've got me. I am the only one who knows what's what around here," Lou said with a grin. She opened a drawer and pulled out an address book. "Here. Try W for Whitepath."

Amy jokingly stuck her tongue out at her sister and flicked through the book. As Lou disappeared back into the kitchen, she found the number and dialled it. To her surprise, she realized that she felt a little nervous.

It was Barbara who answered the phone. "Why, Amy!" she exclaimed. "It's good to hear from you."

Amy instantly remembered Barbara's warmth from her last visit, and how she had served great meals in the cosy log cabin.

"Hi, Barbara," Amy began. "I saw Mercury at a show yesterday, and it made me think of you all at Ten Beeches. I just thought I'd call to say hello and see how you're doing."

"Well, I'm glad you haven't forgotten us," said Barbara. "How are you? Is everything all right at Heartland?"

"Oh, yes. Everything's fine, thanks," said Amy. "It's been a tough year, but we're through all that now." She paused. "Watching Mercury made me remember what an amazing time

15

I had at Ocanumba – and all the things I learned from Huten. Is he there? I'd love to talk to him and tell him how well Mercury is doing."

There was a long silence. Suddenly, Amy wondered if something was wrong, and she could feel her heart start to beat faster. "Barbara?" she prompted.

"I'm sorry, honey," said Barbara in a soft, distant voice. "I'm afraid you can't speak to Huten. He's not … with us any more."

Amy swallowed. "Not with you… You mean…"

Barbara sighed, and Amy noticed that she sounded strained and tired. "Huten died five days ago," she said.

Chapter Two

Amy's body recoiled as though something had hit her. *"Died?"* she echoed.

"It was very sudden," said Barbara. "He'd been ill for a while, but we thought he'd recover. Then … he just went downhill. One minute he was with us, the next he was gone. I'm sorry, Amy."

"No! No, *I'm* sorry," said Amy, gathering her thoughts together. "It must have been a terrible shock for all of you. I – I didn't know." Anguish rose inside her. "I wish I'd called before!" she blurted out.

"None of us saw it coming, Amy," said Barbara, her voice sad but calm.

"Well, thank you for telling me. Please say I'm sorry to Bill and Carey," said Amy. She didn't know what else to say. "I – I'll be in touch again soon."

She put down the phone and sank into the chair, feeling chilled to the bone. Lou came back into the office and found her staring into space, her cup of coffee going cold in front of her.

"Amy! What's wrong?" she exclaimed.

"Huten," whispered Amy. "He's dead, Lou. He died five days ago."

Lou's eyes widened in dismay. She sat down next to Amy and put her arm around her. "I'm so sorry," she murmured.

The two sisters sat in silence for a few moments. Amy felt full of grief and regret. Why had she put off calling them for so long? Time had slipped through her fingers, and now it was too late.

Then Lou spoke. "Do you remember when I drove you to Ocanumba?" she asked softly. "Huten talked about Mom and how she'd promised to return and work with him. But she died before she had the chance. Huten understood that. No one knows when people will be taken from us."

Amy nodded. "He said something else while I was there," she said. "It was an old Native American saying: 'There is no death, only a change of worlds.' He wanted me to keep it in mind, so I would know that Mom was still close. The way he said it, I'm sure he wasn't afraid of dying."

Lou smiled. "Yes," she agreed. "He was an old man, Amy. I guess his time had come."

Amy sighed. "I just wish I'd been able to see him one last time."

They lapsed into silence again. Then Amy rose to her feet. "I'd better get back to work," she said.

"Well ... take it easy," said Lou. "You're allowed to be upset, you know."

Amy nodded and gave a little smile. "Thanks, Lou. I'll be fine."

She took a deep breath and stepped out into the yard.

To Amy's surprise, Joni was leading Spindleberry across the front yard. Amy stopped and watched for a moment. The tall

blonde stable girl was absorbed in teaching the spirited year[ling]
to follow more closely on the lead rope, and didn't see her.

But Spindle did. He turned his head and gave a whinny. Amy
walked over, and Joni looked at her with a friendly smile.

"I was planning to give Spindle a training session myself this
morning," Amy said. She knew she sounded abrupt, but she
couldn't help it. "I've got plenty of time now that school's out."

Joni looked taken aback and was instantly apologetic. "Oh,
Amy, I'm sorry! I didn't know. He just looked so skittish in the
pasture that I thought I'd make the most of his energy..." She
trailed off. "Should I stop and work with one of the other
horses?"

Amy saw the honest question in the other girl's eyes and felt
ashamed. It was great that Joni took so much initiative – it was
one of her best qualities. She blushed slightly. "No, no, it's fine,"
she said. "You keep going. I can work with Shalom. Sorry, I
didn't mean to interfere."

Joni cocked her head to one side. "Are you sure?"

Amy felt even worse. "No. Honestly, Joni, it's fine," she said.
She began to back away. "Really, you're doing a great job. I'll see
you later. I'm going to check in with Ty."

She turned and walked away, trying to seem as if she had a
plan but feeling without direction. *What's the matter with me?* she
asked herself. She trudged down to the far training ring, where
Ty was exercising Sasha, and stood at the fence to watch quietly
for a few moments, trying to put Spindleberry out of her mind.

Sasha was a recent arrival, a beautiful and spirited showjumper
whose owner had been hospitalized after a bad fall. Sasha had

nd to restore her confidence and to keep
r recovered. Ty was lost in concentration
ough her paces, asking her to collect and
headquarters under her, then stretch out her stride
and extend. The harmony between horse and rider once more
reminded Amy of Huten, and how he had almost seemed like
an extension of the horse when he rode, whether bareback or
in the saddle. A lump rose in her throat and her eyes misted
over. She tried to swallow her emotion, then smiled as Ty saw
her and rode over to the fence.

"Is everything OK?" he asked, swinging himself out of the
saddle and looking closely at Amy's face.

"It's Huten, at Ten Beeches," she told him.

Ty unlatched the training ring gate and led Sasha through it.
"Has something happened to him?"

"He's dead," said Amy simply.

Ty stopped in his tracks, his face full of concern. "Oh,
Amy," he said. "I know how important he was to you. Are
you OK?"

Amy nodded. "It's just weird, how things happen," she said.
"You know, like seeing Bruce with Mercury at the show
yesterday. It made me think of Huten and Carey, and that's
probably why I dreamed about Ocanumba last night and then
decided to give them a call. But if it all had happened a week
ago, I might have been in time to talk to him before he – he
was gone."

Ty put his arm around her as they walked back to the yard,
listening as Amy poured out her feelings. "I just wonder how

they're coping without him," she said. "Carey was the only one who helped Huten with problem horses. It's going to be hard for her, taking it all on by herself, and I feel bad that I haven't talked to her in so long. She's really strong, but she'll miss Huten terribly."

Ty squeezed her shoulder. "You could still call her," he said. "It's not too late for that, is it?"

Amy shook her head. "I guess not," she said. "She'll need all the support she can get. The horses will be grieving, too, especially Albatross. Do you remember how Pegasus mourned after Mom died? He was never the same after that."

"Sometimes they get over it, though," Ty pointed out. "Look at Sugarfoot."

Amy thought of the little Shetland, who had become a permanent Heartland resident after the death of his owner, Mrs Bell. At first, Sugarfoot wouldn't even eat. It had been Lou who had brought him out of the depths of his misery by singing to him, just as Mrs Bell had done. Amy smiled at the memory.

"I think Carey would want to talk things through with you," Ty continued. "Don't put off calling just because you wish you'd done it before."

Amy thought about what he said. She was able to relate to Carey's situation. "You're right," she said. "Thanks, Ty. I'll call her in a while."

Later that day, Amy was clearing the dinner table when the phone rang.

Grandpa answered it. "It's for you, Amy," he said, holding out the receiver.

"For me?" She took it from him in surprise.

"Hey, Amy," said the voice at the other end. "I hope you haven't forgotten me."

"Carey!" Amy exclaimed. "Of course I haven't forgotten you. I was just about to call you. I've been thinking about you all day." She hesitated, then blurted out, "Your mom told me about Huten. I'm really sorry."

"Yeah. It's OK, though, you don't have to go all serious on me," said Carey in an offhand tone. "You know, like talk in whispers or anything."

Amy smiled. She had forgotten how defensive Carey could be. "Sure, I understand," she said. "How are the horses doing?"

"They're OK. Dad's got it all under control."

"And ... what about you?" Amy asked hesitantly.

"Me? I'm fine. Maverick's the only issue, really. I don't suppose you remember him."

"Of course I do!" Amy insisted. She'd never forget the little half mustang that Carey and Huten had taken under their wing. He had been badly bullied by other horses but was gradually growing stronger through their reassurance and careful retraining. "I guess he's missing Huten?"

"Oh..." Carey trailed off. "No, it's not that, really."

Amy frowned. The conversation seemed stilted, but she didn't know what to say. Why had Carey called? She didn't seem to want to talk about Huten at all, or how her family was dealing with his being gone.

"Is there anything I can do to help?" Amy asked, feeling at a loss. "I don't know how, but if there's anything—"

"That's kind of why I called," said Carey, suddenly much more assertive. "You could come. Come to Ocanumba."

Amy was startled. "To Ocanumba!" she exclaimed. "Well – I don't know. Like ... when?"

"The sooner the better," said Carey, as though she'd thought it all through.

Amy couldn't get her head around it right away. So much was happening at Heartland. There were the five auction horses as well as all the others, and Joni was still fairly new. "I might be able to," she said cautiously. "But things are pretty busy here. I'm not sure."

"Well, you know where I am," said Carey. "You can let me know when you've made up your mind."

"Right," said Amy. "Sure. I—"

"Thanks," said Carey. "I'll speak to you soon."

Amy put the phone down, feeling mystified. Carey was a complicated person, and it had taken Amy a while to get through to her on her first visit. It was impossible to tell exactly what she wanted now, but Amy knew that the other girl was proud and wouldn't have asked her to visit unless she really meant it. Perhaps she needed help with one of the horses. *It must be difficult for Carey to face working with them on her own*, she thought.

"Well, that was Carey," she said to Lou and Grandpa, who were both at the sink finishing off the dishes. She ran a hand through her hair. "She's asked me to visit Ocanumba."

23

There was a pause. Lou and Jack looked at each other. "It *is* your summer vacation," said Jack, drying his hands on a tea towel. "There's no reason why Heartland can't spare you for a few days."

"What about the five new horses...? I suppose they don't need any special treatment, do they?" added Lou. "Joni seems very capable, and I can always help out in the yard."

"I guess," said Amy. She felt a sudden rush of excitement at the idea of going back to Ten Beeches. It would be so fantastic there at this time of year — summer in the mountains! But then a thought occurred to her. "What about Spindle?" she said out loud.

Lou looked surprised. "Spindle? What about him? He'll be fine for a few days."

She remembered her abrupt reaction to seeing him with Joni that morning, but it was true. Amy didn't know why it should bother her to leave him.

Lou raised one eyebrow. "It won't affect his training that much, will it?"

"No ... not really," Amy admitted sheepishly. She took a deep breath. "Well, I guess I'll need to talk it through with Ty. But thanks. I'd love the chance to go and see Carey and Bill and Barbara."

The next morning, Amy brought in Spindleberry from the pasture, as usual, to begin his morning training session.

"You're going to have to manage without me if I go to Ocanumba," she told him, tying him up in the front yard. She looked into the yearling's dark, trusting eyes as he nuzzled her affectionately. "No early morning treats," she added, when Spindle located some horse cookies in her pocket. "You're getting spoiled!" She laughed as he snuffled at them, then turned round as Joni's little car drove into the yard.

Spindleberry stood still, sniffing the air. When Joni emerged from her car, his ears pricked forward and he gave a whinny.

Joni slammed the driver's door shut and grinned. "Hey, little fella!" she greeted the yearling, coming over to scratch him between his ears. She turned to Amy. "Is everything OK? Should I start with the mucking out?"

Amy smiled and nodded. "Thanks, Joni."

Joni headed to the barn, and Amy watched her go. Lou was right. Now that Joni was around, there really wasn't any reason why she shouldn't go to Ocanumba. And in a flash of honesty, it dawned on her that she wasn't at all worried about how the other girl would cope if she were to leave Heartland for a few days. It was actually the reverse. With her many skills and tireless commitment, Joni would handle everything all too well.

Chapter Three

"Libby's a lot less jumpy than she was the last time we took her on the trails," Amy commented as she and Ty rode side by side up the steep incline to Clairdale Ridge. Ty was riding the grey mare, while Amy was on the gentle bay gelding, Bear.

"Yeah. She still spooks at the sound of cars, though," said Ty. "She won't be road-safe for a while yet."

"Poor girl," murmured Amy. "Who can blame her?"

They rode along at a relaxed pace, walking and trotting, until they reached the top of the ridge. Looking out over the view reminded Amy of Ocanumba, with its tree-covered mountainsides, and she turned to Ty. She'd put off speaking to him about her visit up until now. She felt bad that she'd be leaving him again so soon after her trip to visit her father in Australia – but she had an idea that she hoped would make the trip fun for both of them.

"I spoke to Carey last night," she began.

"That's good. How is she?"

Amy frowned. "I couldn't really tell," she admitted. "I think she's feeling pretty down. Actually –" she paused before finishing in a rush – "she invited me to go there for a few days, and I was wondering if you'd mind giving me a ride?"

Ty looked thoughtful. "Wow!" he said. "That's some trip."

"Well, it could be fun," said Amy. "It's a pretty route, and we haven't ever really taken a road trip like that."

Ty thought for a few more moments, then seemed to make up his mind. "Sure. I guess Joni can hold the fort here for a few days, and I haven't had any real time off since my accident. It'd be great to get away together."

Amy stared at him uncertainly. Was Ty suggesting that he'd *stay* at Ten Beeches? When Grandpa had driven her to Ocanumba last time, he'd driven back home again the same day.

"There isn't a problem, is there?" asked Ty, seeing her expression.

Amy shrugged. "It's just…" She trailed off. "Well, we can't both leave Heartland, can we?"

Ty's face fell, and Amy instantly regretted her words. She'd already been away on one amazing trip this year, yet here she was planning another! And she couldn't really argue that Joni was too new to leave alone. She'd faced up to that in the yard.

But Carey had invited Amy as a personal friend. She hadn't mentioned anyone else. "Actually, it's not that," she said hurriedly. "I was just thinking that Carey only invited me. It might be kind of awkward, that's all."

That sounded just as bad. Ty's expression was difficult to read, and Amy guessed that he was trying to hide his hurt. When he spoke, it was clear that he was choosing his words carefully. "Well," he said, "I guess you'd need to check with her first. Even if I can't stay over, I'll drive you there anyway." He paused, looking apologetic. "It's just that it's a long way to drive there and back."

Amy felt worse and worse. Ty had almost completely

recovered from his accident, but he still found it tiring to drive for long periods of time. "Ty, I'm sorry," she said. "I'll ask Carey. I'm sure it'll be fine."

Ty studied her. "If you're sure it's what you want," he said. "I know we don't usually leave Heartland together, but Joni's really good. She'll get along perfectly with help from Lou and Jack."

"I know," Amy said, forcing a smile. "Well, I'll talk to Carey tonight."

They rode back down the trail in silence. Amy's thoughts were racing. She realized that she'd been looking forward to visiting Ocanumba on her own, knowing that Ty would have everything under control at Heartland. And Carey's invitation meant a lot to her. On her first visit, it had taken a while to break the ice with the other girl, but once she had, they'd developed a very deep friendship.

At the time, Carey had been about to leave Ocanumba. She had decided that life in the mountains was no longer for her and that she needed to get away from the family traditions. But Amy had seen Carey's amazing skill with horses and how closely she resembled Huten. When Carey had shown her parts of the forest that had been lived in by her ancestors, Amy had begun to understand the other girl's history and to question her reasons for leaving it behind.

Through their honest discussions, Carey had realized that she should stay and work alongside her grandfather. In return, she had helped Amy to understand the way Huten worked, and how she could reach Mercury. It had all been very special, and

Amy felt that it wouldn't be the same with someone else around, even if that person was Ty.

Back at Heartland, Amy turned out Libby and Bear in the top pasture before heading indoors for a late lunch. As she investigated leftovers in the fridge, Lou and Nancy chatted over coffee at the kitchen table. Much to Lou's relief, Nancy had jumped at the idea of helping with the wedding catering.

"Typical fall food – simple and wholesome," Nancy was saying. "Two or three hearty casseroles, a couple of pies and lots of root vegetables – pumpkins, roast potatoes, glazed carrots and squash. Everyone will love it."

Lou nodded enthusiastically. "And it's practically foolproof," she added. "Unless we burn everything."

"Impossible," said Nancy with a smile as Amy sat down to join them with a slice of cold pizza. "All they need is a little care and attention and they'll cook themselves."

Lou flashed a knowing grin at Amy, and she smiled back. Her sister's plans were beginning to come together, and Amy felt glad for her. She was looking forward to the wedding, too, though at that moment she was more preoccupied with the trip to Ocanumba. She munched the pizza and half listened to the catering plans, hoping that she hadn't offended Ty.

Nancy got up to clear the coffee cups, and Lou turned to Amy. "How was your morning?" she asked. "Did you talk to Ty about going to Ten Beeches?"

Amy nodded. "I asked him to drive me there," she said in a low voice. She hesitated, not really wanting to discuss the issue in front of Nancy. "And he wants to stay there, too."

Lou cocked her head to one side. "Well, I guess that might be OK."

Amy looked at Lou pleadingly, hoping she'd understand. "I don't think we should both leave the horses, but Ty thinks it's OK."

Lou's eyebrows shot up. "Ah," she said. "I see." She touched Amy's arm as Nancy gathered up the rest of the dirty dishes. "We'll talk about it later, all right?"

Amy worked in the back barn for the rest of the day, giving the stalls a thorough mucking out and replacing all the bedding while the horses were grazing. In the summer months, it was much easier to fit everything in. Not only was she not at school, the horses needed less stable care, too.

She finished just as the sun was setting. Ty and Joni headed home for the evening, and Amy went indoors. She had just changed out of her yard clothes when her sister appeared at her bedroom door.

"So what's all this about Ty and Ten Beeches?" Lou asked, her arms crossed over her chest.

Amy finished buttoning her shirt and sighed. "I feel really bad, Lou. I asked Ty if he'd drive me to Ocanumba, and he assumed I meant for him to *stay* there."

"Well, like I said, that seems like a good idea to me." Lou looked shrewdly at Amy. "But you don't think so?"

Amy chewed her lip. She wasn't sure how open to be about how she'd been feeling. She didn't want to admit that she wanted Carey and Ten Beeches all to herself ... or how much it bothered her that Joni was bonding with Spindle. "It feels wrong to leave the place just to Joni," she said at last. "I know that you and Grandpa can help…" She shrugged.

"So how did you leave things with Ty?" Lou came into the room and sat on Amy's bed.

"I said I'd ask Carey," said Amy. "It was kind of difficult. I don't want to hurt anyone's feelings." She dragged a brush through her hair while Lou frowned and sat thinking for a few minutes.

"You know, Heartland really would be fine for a few days without you and Ty," she said. "But I get the feeling that's not really the issue. You're afraid that something will change while you're away, aren't you?"

Amy stared at her. "Change? Like – how?"

Lou gave a little smile. "We've never had someone like Joni around before," she pointed out. "Ben was great, but even I can see that Joni is much happier using our natural remedies. It must feel pretty strange, knowing we have someone who can do the same work as you and Ty."

Amy nodded. It was true. She'd already acknowledged it to herself. "I guess," she admitted, feeling guilty.

"Well, I don't think you have to worry about Joni taking over completely," said Lou. "A few days never changed anything."

She paused, and Amy could bear it no longer. "Actually, it's not just that," she blurted out. "The thing is, Carey hasn't invited Ty. She only invited me. But I felt awful telling him that."

Lou looked surprised. "Ah, right," she said. "That's different."

"Yes." Amy waited in suspense while Lou thought it through.

"Well, it's true that Ty can't just show up," said her sister eventually. "You'll have to check it out with the Whitepaths first."

"But … it's more than that," said Amy anxiously. "I mean, last time I went on my own. It'll be different if Ty's there."

Lou smiled gently. "It's going to be different anyway, Amy," she said. "If the Whitepaths say yes, I think you'll be really glad Ty's there with you. Huten's not around any more, remember? The whole family is in mourning. You might need some support."

Lou's words made sense, and Amy played miserably with her hairbrush, feeling ashamed that she hadn't thought about the situation more carefully. "You're right," she admitted. "I just wish I hadn't made things so awkward with Ty."

Lou stood up and went to the door. "Don't worry about what's already been said," she told her. "You can still fix things."

Amy smiled at her sister. "You're right, Lou," she said. "I'll call Ten Beeches after dinner and check if it's OK for Ty to come with me."

When she called later, it was Barbara who answered the phone, and Amy was glad to hear her sounding more cheerful than she had the last time she'd spoken to her.

"Hi, Amy!" Barbara greeted her. "Carey tells me you might be coming to stay. That's just great. You're more than welcome."

"Well, thank you," said Amy. "I'd love to come. There's just one thing I need to ask you."

"Of course," Barbara said.

Amy took a deep breath. "It's just that my boyfriend, Ty, will be driving me to Ocanumba, and it's a pretty long trip. We were wondering how you'd feel about him staying, too?"

"No problem at all. What a good idea!" exclaimed Barbara. She paused. "You know, Amy, we all need friends at times like this. It's not easy for Carey, living here with just Bill and me. We'd be delighted if both of you came."

Instantly Amy began to feel better. "Thanks, Barbara," she said. "Well, I guess all we need to do is work out some dates and get back to you. I'm really looking forward to it. It was so special, visiting you last time."

She put the phone down with a sigh of relief. But as she left the kitchen, she felt another pang of doubt. Should she have spoken to Carey as well as Barbara? It was all very well for Barbara to be welcoming, but the visit hadn't been *her* idea. It would have made more sense to check with Carey first.

Well, it was too late now. She couldn't call back and tell Barbara that she needed to check with Carey. She'd have to go through with the plans as they stood and hope for the best.

She told Ty first thing in the morning as they were measuring out the feeds. "So all we need to do is decide when to go," she finished.

Ty's face broke into a grin. "We'll have a great time, I promise," he said. He looked at her questioningly. "Don't you think?"

"Sure," she agreed. She looked up at him, trying to shake off

33

any doubts she had about his coming. "I'm sorry about yesterday," she said softly. "I didn't want you to feel that you weren't welcome."

"That's OK," said Ty. "I've already forgotten."

He turned back to the feeds and handed Amy one of the buckets. She was just about to head out with it when they heard Joni cry out.

"Spindle! What happened to you?"

Chapter Four

Amy rushed out into the yard and cannoned into Joni, who was jogging towards the feed room. "Is he OK?" she demanded.

"He's fine. Don't worry, I'll take care of it," Joni called over her shoulder, disappearing inside the feed room. As Amy ran to Spindleberry's stall, she thought back to when she had brought him in the night before. She had wanted to make sure he got his weekly dose of liver tonic, so she put it in his water and planned to keep him in his stall until he drank the bucket dry. She remembered him looking at her as she closed the stall door. He had seemed fine then.

Amy struggled with the sliding bolt, and Spindle raised his head at the sound. He gave a welcoming whinny when he saw her, as usual, and Amy felt instant relief, but then she looked at his shoulder. The hair was matted with blood, and a sticky red trail ran down his foreleg.

Amy's stomach lurched. "Spindle!" she said, and gasped. Hurriedly, she let herself into the stall and examined him. There was a jagged cut on his shoulder about two inches long. Amy looked around for what might have caused it. It didn't take long to figure it out. Restless and curious as ever, Spindle had nibbled at his manger and tugged it away from the wall, exposing a couple of sharp screws.

"Come here, let me see," said Amy as the yearling jostled

her. He seemed untroubled by his injury, which was good news, at least. And once she had taken a closer look at the wound, Amy could see that it was only superficial, and it had already stopped bleeding. She looked up as Joni reappeared at the stall door, carrying a basin of hot water and some treatments.

"It's not serious," Amy told her. "I'd just disinfect it, then give him a few drops of Rescue Remedy for the shock and wipe on some arnica to help the bruising."

Joni smiled and showed Amy what she was holding – exactly the things she had mentioned. "That's what I thought, too," she said, putting the basin down. "The only thing I'm worried about is tetanus."

"Oh, that's OK," said Amy. "Scott inoculated the auction horses when we decided to keep them, so they're all up to date with their shots."

She watched as Joni wiped the wound with wads of damp cotton, itching to do it herself. But she could see there was no need. Joni knew what she was doing, and all Amy could do was soothe the yearling as the other girl applied some disinfectant cream. Amy looked up as Ty appeared at the entrance.

"Is everything OK?" he asked, leaning on the half-door.

Amy nodded and gave him a quick smile. As Joni dabbed some arnica on the area around the wound, Amy thought of what Lou had said the night before. *It must feel pretty strange, knowing we have someone who can do the same work as you and Ty.* Yes, it did feel strange. Joni was capable, willing, easy to be around – and she knew a lot of the Heartland methods already. Amy felt almost ashamed of herself for feeling threatened by her efficiency. Joni was exactly what they'd been looking for! Why should Amy resent that?

"There," said Joni, putting the lid back on the arnica tube. "All done. He'll be fine now!"

"Yeah, I guess so," Amy said. "You were great, Joni. I don't know what we'd do without you!" She shot a quick look at Ty and decided that now would be a good moment to mention their plans. "Actually, we needed to talk to you about something."

"Oh? What's up?" Joni looked from Amy to Ty and back again.

"Ty and I are going away for a few days," Amy explained, still feeling a little hesitant. "I need to see a friend of mine up in the Appalachians, and Ty's going to drive us there. We're sure you'll be able to manage here without us, if that's OK with you."

Joni's eyes widened. "Wow," she said.

"You won't be on your own," Ty put in. "Lou and Jack will be around, of course, and we can ask Ben to be on hand to help with some of the stable chores if they get to be too much."

Joni cleared her throat, looking a little overwhelmed, but pleased. "Thank you, Amy," she said. "I can't believe you'd give me that much responsibility. It means a lot to me."

Amy played with Spindle's mane, blushing a bit from Joni's gratitude. "We trust you," she said simply.

Just then Spindle turned away and ran his teeth along the edge of the damaged manger again. "No, you don't!" cried Joni as she and Amy jumped to pull him away. Ty chuckled as he looked on. Joni looked at Amy and rolled her eyes. "I'll keep a close eye on Spindle, I promise. Something tells me he's going to need it!"

Two days later, Amy and Ty loaded their bags into the back of his pickup, ready for their trip. Grandpa and Nancy, Lou and Joni stood in the yard and waved as Ty and Amy climbed inside. Ty started up the engine.

Amy lowered her window and leaned out. "See you next week!" she called as they started down the drive.

"Drive safely! Have a great time," called Grandpa.

"Don't worry about anything!" Joni added.

Amy settled back into her seat and smiled at Ty. "We're off," she said, feeling a sudden rush of excitement. Now that they were packed and on their way, all her doubts – about leaving Heartland, about Ty coming – were put to rest. It seemed pointless to dwell on her worries when it was such a beautiful day – sunny but not too hot, just perfect for a drive in the mountains. Ty drove steadily for a couple of hours before pulling in to a diner for some lunch. As he and Amy sat down to burgers and Cokes, Amy began to think about the horses at Ten Beeches.

"It's too bad you didn't get more time to look around last time," she commented. Ty had come with Grandpa to pick her up and had only met the Whitepaths briefly. "You didn't see Maverick, did you?"

Ty shook his head and took a bite of his burger.

"Maverick's the only horse that Carey mentioned on the phone," Amy went on. "He's half mustang. Huten rescued him from a really awful homestead, where there hadn't been enough grazing and he'd been badly bullied by the other horses. I'm sure they did a fantastic job with him, but Carey says there's some kind of issue with him now. I think that's what she wants me to help with, but I'm not certain."

"Could be anything, I guess," said Ty. "If Carey's at all like you, their yard will be full of horses needing help!"

"That's true," Amy agreed, feeling more excited by the minute.

"Well, it won't be long until you find out," said Ty. "Once we get back on the road, we should be there in a couple more hours!"

As the road wound up through the foothills of the Appalachian Mountains, Amy's memories of Ten Beeches came rushing back – the scent of pine needles through the pickup's open windows, the fresh, clean air, and the glimpses of sparkling rivulets running down the hillsides. None of it had changed. When they turned up the driveway that led to Ten Beeches, she felt invigorated. She waved eagerly at Bill and Barbara, who were waiting for them outside their log cabin.

"Welcome back!" cried Barbara as Amy opened her door.

"It's good to be here," said Amy, smiling. Barbara and Bill hugged her in turn. They were just as Amy remembered them – Bill was tall, gentle and jovial, while Barbara was small and dark-haired with warm, smiling eyes.

"You remember Ty, don't you?" Amy asked as Ty stepped out of the pickup.

Bill shook Ty's hand heartily. "Of course we do," he said. "Though we're glad we'll be seeing more of him this time!"

"Now, come on inside," said Barbara. "I'll show you your rooms. Do you need a hand with your stuff?"

"We're fine," said Amy, hoisting her backpack on to her shoulder as Ty grabbed his suitcase. "We didn't bring much."

"Travel light, travel easy – that's what Huten used to say," said Barbara, leading them indoors.

Amy felt relieved that Barbara had been the first to mention Huten, and with such ease. It was hard to believe that he wasn't going to appear suddenly around the stable block or at the cabin door. Amy fought down a wave of sadness. She entered the cosy little cabin. It was just as before – the beautiful textile hangings, the wood-burning stove, the enticing smell of Barbara's cooking. It was such a welcoming place that Amy instantly felt her spirits lift.

Barbara ushered them through the kitchen and to the spare room at the back of the house. "You'll be in here," she told Amy.

"Just like last time," said Amy, looking around the small, familiar room with its chest and wardrobe, both painted eggshell blue. "Thanks, Barbara. I love this room."

"And you'll be up in the attic, Ty," said Barbara. "It's a little cramped, but it has a nice view of the yard. I hope you don't mind."

"Sounds great," Ty said with a grin.

Amy watched as Barbara showed Ty the steps that led to his room. There was one question: where was Carey? Why hadn't she come to welcome them, too? For some reason, Amy didn't want to ask. Barbara and Bill seemed so relaxed and cheerful – much more than Amy might have expected, given Huten's recent death – that it seemed thoughtless to raise any doubts about Carey's behaviour.

Amy and Ty had agreed to meet outside in a few minutes. They walked down the little wood-chip path that led from the cabin to the yard. There were two long rows of stalls facing each other and another block along one end, so the yard formed a large T, and in the middle of the end block there was a small wooden cabin that housed the tack and feed rooms.

A bronzed man of about thirty-five peered out of one of the stalls. When he saw them, he leaned over the half-door and watched them approach. Amy didn't recognize him and guessed that he hadn't been at Ten Beeches when she last visited.

"May I help you?" he asked politely. His almond-shaped eyes were such a dark brown that they were nearly black, and his long dark hair was pulled back in a ponytail.

"We're looking for Bill," Amy said. "Is he around?"

The man frowned. "There aren't any rides going out this afternoon, I'm afraid."

"Oh, we're not here for a ride," said Amy. "We're friends of the family. We're staying at the house."

"Gee, I'm sorry," said the man. "You must be Amy, right? Bill did tell me you were coming. I forgot it was today." He held out his hand. "I'm Aiden. I help Bill with the trail-ride business."

"Hi, Aiden," said Amy, shaking hands. "Nice to meet you. This is Ty."

Aiden smiled and vigorously shook hands with Ty. "Bill's doing the evening feeds. He'll be around somewhere. Try the feed room," he suggested, pointing.

As Aiden disappeared back into the stall, Amy and Ty spotted Bill carrying a feed bucket. They waved and headed over.

"So you met Aiden," said Bill. "Nice fellow, eh? I've nearly finished the feeds. Why don't you take a look around? I'll join you in a minute."

Amy and Ty wandered up the longer row of stalls, looking in at the horses munching their evening feeds. Amy had got the sense from Huten and Carey that they dealt with some extreme cases in the treatment practice – horses that were deprived and battered, like Maverick. However, Amy did not see any horses that fit that bill. They all seemed to be tough, sturdy specimens, and Amy guessed from the sheen on their coats and the grain in their feed that most of them were being used for Bill's trail-riding business. If they had come to Ten Beeches for treatment, they wouldn't need as much feed in the summer months when they could be turned out in the pasture, and they probably wouldn't look so healthy and relaxed.

"Looks like they're mainly trail horses," she commented to Ty. "I wonder what's happened to the treatment side? I don't see any signs of it. And there are empty stalls."

"Maybe they've had to cut back," said Ty.

Amy frowned. "Carey didn't say anything about that."

They stopped at a stall where a big, muscular paint horse was pulling at a hay net. He turned his head to look at them, and Amy recognized his handsome face at once.

"Albatross!" she whispered. "Ty, it's Huten's old horse. The one I told you about."

Albatross flicked his ears at the sound of Amy's voice. His intelligent eyes looked curious, and he left his hay to investigate his new visitors. It was clear that he was in the peak of condition, with his black-and-white coat gleaming and his white mane flowing gracefully over the arch of his neck. Amy reached up and stroked his nose, a lump forming in her throat as memories of Huten flooded back. Seeing Huten ride Albatross bareback without even a bridle to direct him had filled Amy with awe – she had never witnessed such a natural connection. Watching them, the traditional roles of horse and rider seemed archaic. Huten and Albatross were bonded, and their partnership was on a higher plain. *Poor Albatross*, Amy thought. *You must miss Huten so much.*

But Albatross pricked his ears and took an eager step towards them, sniffing both Amy and Ty. Amy studied his face with a growing feeling of surprise. His big dark eyes were calm and bright, and as he lipped gently at Ty's fingers, she could see that there was no tension around his muzzle. This wasn't a horse in deep mourning – quite the opposite, in fact.

"He seems to be in good spirits," said Ty, echoing her thoughts.

"Doesn't he?" Amy agreed. She thought of her mom's horse, Pegasus, and how he had suffered after Marion had died. It was puzzling that Albatross seemed so relaxed. "Well, maybe it hasn't hit him yet," she said sadly. "He might not realize that Huten's not coming back."

When Albatross decided to return to his hay, Amy and Ty moved to the last stall in the block and peered in. A slender dun-coloured pony peered back through his forelock, and Amy turned to Ty. "Here he is," she said. "Maverick."

"Hello, boy," Ty greeted him, leaning over the door.

Maverick flared his nostrils and put his ears back, then pivoted away. He swung his hindquarters round so that his head was in the shadow of the stall.

"Oh my," said Amy, raising her eyebrows. "Far from the friendly greeting we got from Albatross. I guess he's never going to be a member of the welcome wagon, after what he's been through."

Ty gazed at the little horse. "I love mustangs," he murmured. "Maverick looks nothing like Dazzle, but there's still something that reminds me of him. Maybe it's because he's so gutsy, like he's totally capable of taking care of himself. Dazzle was like that, too."

Amy smiled. Dazzle was a wild stallion that had come to Heartland for gentling. The stallion had played a big role in Ty's recovery from his accident, and the two of them had formed a close bond. It had been tough for Ty when Dazzle returned to his home, and for a while Amy had wondered if Ty should have a horse of his own – after all, she had Sundance and now, Spindleberry. But Ty had assured her that he wanted to focus all his attention on the different horses that came to Heartland for treatment.

Amy was surprised when Ty let himself into Maverick's stall. She watched quietly by the door, observing the horse's reaction. Maverick backed away at once, with his ears flat against his head. Ty waited for a few moments until he seemed calmer, then took another step into the stall, holding out his fingers for the half mustang to sniff.

Maverick glared at him, flashing the whites of his eyes.

"He looks kind of afraid," said Amy, puzzled, wondering if Ty might decide to back out. Maverick had clearly come a long way since her last visit. His flanks had filled out and he looked healthy and well cared for. But even so, with Huten and Carey's attention, she'd have expected him to have grown more relaxed.

Ty nodded and remained motionless for a while, still holding out his hand towards Maverick. Slowly, the little horse stretched his nose to blow over Ty's fingers. Ty stroked his muzzle, and Amy saw the tense lines of the horse's body begin to soften.

Just as Ty was reaching up to stroke Maverick's neck, Bill appeared and stood at the door next to Amy.

"I see you've found Maverick," he said. "Maverick by name, maverick by nature."

Amy smiled and watched as the half mustang allowed Ty to scratch his withers. "He's in much better shape than he was last time I came," she said. "He was so thin before. But he still seems pretty timid. Is he OK?"

"Oh, he's fine," said Bill, rather hurriedly. He gave an awkward smile. "He's not too fond of visitors, that's all. Myself included."

Ty glanced in Bill's direction and gave Maverick a final pat before coming over to the door.

"Are you treating many horses at the moment?" asked Amy as Ty let himself out of the stall. "It looks as though you've got more trail horses now."

Bill nodded. "Yes. We've really cut back on the treatment work. We had to when Huten became sick. It was too much for Carey, and I couldn't do both lines of work. I decided to concentrate on the trail rides – I hate to say it, but they've always paid better. Barbara had to give up her work to look after Huten." He shrugged. "We didn't have much choice."

"I'm sorry," said Amy. She really meant it. Perhaps if she'd known what was happening, she might have been able to help. She could understand that Huten's work was a lot for Carey to take on. But with some support from Heartland, even just at the other end of the phone, her friend might have found it easier.

"What will happen once things have settled down?" Ty asked. "Will you build the treatment side up again?"

Bill looked thoughtful. "I guess it's an option," he said. "Barbara's gone back to work part-time at the housing project now. A lot will depend on Carey and – well, I daresay she'll tell you all about that herself."

Carey. She *still* hadn't even made an appearance, Amy realized. Amy looked around the yard, wondering where her elusive friend might be.

"You were doing well with Maverick," Bill told Ty. "He's quite a handful – too unpredictable for tourists."

"So you don't take him out on trail rides?" asked Ty.

Bill shook his head. "I don't use him at all, not even for

myself. Unfortunately, that means he's not earning his keep. Things are pretty tight here now, you know. It's been a tough decision to make, but Maverick's going to have to find a new home."

Chapter Five

Amy spun round to face Bill, shocked. "A new home!" she exclaimed. "You mean you're going to sell him?"

"That's right," said Bill. "Didn't Carey tell you?"

Amy shook her head. "No, she didn't mention it." Then again, Carey hadn't said much about anything. Was this the reason Carey had wanted her to come? Amy realized she had no clue as to what Carey's motives were. "Where is she?" Amy asked, feeling frustrated.

Bill gave a lopsided smile. "You know our Carey," he said. "She's around here somewhere. Why don't you two walk to the pastures? You might find her there."

"OK, thanks. We'll do that," said Amy, striving to sound more lighthearted. "Are you sure you don't need any help here first?"

"No, no, there aren't any more rides this afternoon, and Aiden's here now," Bill assured her. "I have to do some paperwork anyway, so you head off and relax. You've had a long trip. Supper's at seven — that's all you need to know."

As Amy and Ty walked down to the paddocks, the shadow of the mountain was lengthening, casting shadows across the dirt track. They came to a training ring on their left, and Amy stopped.

"This is where I first saw Huten riding Albatross," she said.

"It was amazing, Ty. It's hard to believe he's gone. Seeing them that day, I would have thought they'd be together for ever."

Ty put his arm around her. "His not being around sure seems to have changed things," he agreed. "But it's good to be here. I'm glad I came."

Thinking of how she had dealt with it, Amy felt a shiver of guilt at his words. She still wasn't sure how she felt about him staying. For some reason, it didn't seem the same with him there. Her first trip had been such a revelation – it had felt like an adventure – but she pushed the thought aside for now. They continued down the path towards the big pasture, and suddenly there was Carey. She was sitting on the fence, watching them as they walked towards her. She looked as though she were expecting them. Her small, wiry frame and dark features were so reminiscent of Huten's that, for a moment, Amy felt tears welling up in her eyes.

"Carey!" she called, after swallowing hard. "How's it going?"

Carey didn't move or wave back. When Amy and Ty reached her, Carey gave Ty a cool, appraising look. "Hi, Amy," she said.

"You remember Ty, don't you?" asked Amy. Her cheeks had grown hot at the girl's indifference. She seemed to be deliberately ignoring Ty.

"Sure. Hi, Ty," Carey responded coolly.

Amy shot a look at Ty. She noticed the surprise in his eyes, then saw him quickly mask it. *I was right*, she thought. *This was a bad idea.*

"Hi, Carey," Ty said, with a broad smile. "Good to meet you again. I've heard a lot about you."

Carey shrugged and looked down at a piece of grass she was twisting in her hands. Amy felt embarrassed. Perhaps Huten's death had affected Carey more than she had let on. Carey had every reason to be feeling down. But there was no need to be rude, was there?

"I think I'll go and finish unpacking my things," Ty said awkwardly. "You guys have a lot of catching up to do."

Amy and Carey watched in silence as Ty made his way back up the path. When he disappeared between the trees, Amy wondered what she should do. Part of her wanted to run after Ty and apologize for Carey's behaviour. At the same time, she guessed that Carey must be feeling pretty awful to have acted that way. Maybe it would be best to get some time alone with her.

"Are you OK?" Amy asked at last.

"I'm fine, thanks. Are you?"

"Yes, I'm fine." Amy paused, frantically trying to think of something that would break the ice. "Your dad was telling us about Maverick," she said. "He said you're going to sell him." She hoped Carey wouldn't think she was being tactless, bringing this up so soon.

Carey glanced at Amy, then gave a derisive snort. "I think Dad's being optimistic," she said in a scornful tone. "No one will buy Maverick."

Amy stared at her. Did Carey want to sell the horse or not? There was so much smouldering emotion beneath her friend's words that Amy didn't know what to say. Was she concerned about Maverick, or was she grieving for Huten? Or could it be something else entirely? Amy took a deep breath.

"Look," she said carefully. "If there's a problem with Maverick, Ty and I are more than willing to help. If we can, that is. That's why we came."

Carey gave Amy an incredulous look. "That's very generous of you, Amy. But, to be honest, it's not my fault if Maverick doesn't like being yanked and pulled and kicked around by strangers." She jumped off the fence and started marching back up the path.

Stunned, Amy watched as Carey disappeared towards the log cabin before slowly following her. She kicked stones along the dirt path, considering what her friend had said. Carey's words were dismissive, as though she had no connection with the little mustang. Yet Amy remembered that she had mentioned him on the phone. It didn't make sense. She decided to go inside and found Ty in the main room, looking at the bookcase. He gave her a curious look. "Hi. Is everything OK?"

Amy shrugged. "She wasn't open to much more conversation after you left, if that's what you mean. I'm sorry she was so rude to you."

"That's not your fault. She's upset about her grandfather."

"Yeah," Amy said uncomfortably, knowing that she might be partially to blame. Carey's hostility had been partly directed at Ty, and Amy had never told her that she would be bringing a friend along.

Just then, Barbara peered around the door. "Ah! You're both here," she said. "Supper's ready. I hope you're hungry!"

Ty and Amy headed to the kitchen, where the table was set and the smell of lemon and fresh fish filled the air. Bill was washing his hands at the sink, and as Barbara started to serve the meal, Carey sidled in without a word and sat down next to Amy.

"We're having trout," Barbara told them, placing a fillet of fish on each plate. "Freshly caught by one of our friends, I'm proud to say! There's more in the pan, so tuck in."

When everyone had helped themselves to mashed potatoes and green beans, Amy looked around the table. Bill and Barbara were making an effort to talk to Ty about Heartland, while Carey concentrated on her food, barely raising her head. Was she imagining it, Amy wondered, or was there tension in the air? Then she caught Barbara throwing her daughter a look of concern and realized that she wasn't the only one who was finding Carey difficult at the moment. There was definitely something wrong, but unless Carey started to relax and open up, Amy didn't know how she could find out what it was.

The next morning, Ty and Amy both rose at their usual early hour. Breakfast was Barbara's delicious home-made waffles, and when they'd had their fill they headed out to the stable yard. Amy wondered if Carey had got up to help her father with the horses, but there was no sign of her. They found Bill on his own, sluicing down the yard with a hose.

"Can we help?" Ty offered.

"No, no, that's not what you're here for," said Bill. "Why don't you take a couple of the horses and go on to the trails?" He smiled at Amy. "You could show Ty some of the places you visited with Huten."

Amy felt a twinge of exasperation. She was not at all certain why she was there, but it wasn't to take Ty on a trail ride around the sights. Carey had invited her there for some reason, and it was Carey she needed to find.

"Well, that would be great," said Ty, before she could respond. "But are you sure we can't help?"

"Absolutely," said Bill. "Aiden will be here soon." He turned off the hose and began winding it up. "If you give me a few minutes, I'll saddle up a couple of horses for you."

Feeling frustrated, Amy realized she was going to have to resign herself to the trip. "Don't worry about that," she said politely. "We can tack them up if you point us in the right direction."

Ty nodded in agreement. "Could one of us ride Maverick?" he asked.

Bill's forehead creased into a frown. "Maverick?" he echoed doubtfully. He shook his head. "That's not such a great idea, you know. I know you're both experienced, but I'd rather give you horses I can rely on."

In spite of herself, Amy caught Ty's eye. She could tell that his curiosity was aroused just as much as hers. It seemed odd, and very sad, that after all this time the little horse was still battling the same demons.

"I was just about to turn him out for the day, as a matter of fact," Bill went on. "A lot of fun that'll be. For some reason, I seem to be his least favourite person."

Suppressing all the questions that flooded into her mind,

Amy followed Bill to Maverick's stall. She and Ty stood at the door and watched as Bill entered and slipped a halter over the mustang's head. Maverick's ears flattened, and he lunged for Bill's arm with his teeth.

"Hey! Enough of that," Bill scolded. He clipped a lead rope on to the halter and opened the stall door wide, then clicked his tongue to coax Maverick outside. The little horse resisted at every step, glaring at Bill and dragging his feet. Once out in the daylight, Amy could see that he had broken into a sweat.

"I know the little fella's had problems," said Bill, clearly frustrated. "I'm not blaming him for acting up, but he needs a lot of time and attention, and time's the one thing I just don't have any more. Come on, Mav."

Now that he had the space to move, Maverick scooted backwards, his eyes rolling as his hooves scraped over the concrete.

"Look," said Ty, stepping forward. "We're used to horses like this. We work with them every day. You're busy, Bill. Why don't you let us get him down to the pasture? We can take our time and let him calm down a bit."

A mixture of guilt and relief passed over Bill's face, and he hesitated. "I don't know..." he said. "But it definitely would save me some time. Are you guys sure you can handle it?"

"Yes," chorused Amy and Ty.

"Well, thanks," said Bill, handing Ty the lead rope. "I'll get those trail horses ready for when you get back."

Left to their own devices, Amy and Ty waited for the half mustang to calm down before trying to walk him forward.

Maverick eyed them suspiciously, his ears still laid back and his head held high. But when Ty began to massage him in T-touch circles up his neck, Amy saw the pony begin to relax. She was murmuring to him and stroking his nose when she heard a vehicle come up the driveway and a car door slam. A couple of minutes later, Aiden appeared on the yard and raised his hand in greeting.

"Hi, there," he called, and grinned. "I see Bill's got you working. Well, that's one job I don't mind leaving to you. Old Mav's a handful, that's for sure."

Amy instinctively smiled at Aiden's good-natured remark, but inside she felt sad. Nobody at the yard seemed to have much time for the troubled little horse. She watched as Aiden went to the feed room and emerged with two hay nets slung over his shoulder. The daily routine was getting under way, and Maverick clearly wasn't part of it.

"I think we could try getting him to the pasture now," said Ty after a few more minutes.

Amy nodded and gave the lead rope a little tug. Maverick resisted, but only half-heartedly. He took a few steps forward and, with further encouragement, slowly walked to the paddock. When Amy opened the gate and unclipped the rope, the little horse leaped away from them at once and trotted off. Then, when he was at a safe distance, he turned to stare back at them with dark and unreadable eyes before dropping his head to graze.

Back at the yard, Bill had been as good as his word. Two horses awaited them, fully tacked up – a sprightly chestnut mare of about fifteen hands and a handsome grey gelding. "Thanks for doing that," Bill said as he led the horses over.

"I'm glad we could help," said Amy. "So who are these two?"

"Brandy for you," Bill announced to Amy, indicating the chestnut. "And the grey for Ty. His name's Rugged Glen, but we just call him Glen."

Amy and Ty climbed into the elegant, high-pommelled Western saddles and gathered up their reins. Although they rode English-style at Heartland, it wouldn't take either of them long to get used to the longer stirrups and more casual style of Western riding. "Could you tell us how to get down to the village, then back along the mountain stream?" asked Amy.

Bill smiled. "I can do better than that," he said, pulling a pencil and a scrunched-up piece of paper from his pocket. He quickly sketched a rough map and held it out to Amy. "You can't really get lost around here," he said. "Not if you stay on the paths. Have a good ride. I might bump into you – I'll be headed that way with a ride later on. I have a tour group coming, and they want to go to the village."

Glancing at the simple map, Amy recalled the general layout of the trails. She thanked Bill, then she and Ty nudged their horses forward. As they clattered out of the yard, Amy cast a final glance around for Carey. It felt odd to be heading out for the day without even saying hello. But there was still no sign of her, so she slid the reins along Brandy's neck and the horse veered to a shady path that led downhill through the woods.

The path was wide enough for them to ride side by side, and once they were well into the shade of the tall old trees, Amy let her frustration spill out.

"It doesn't make sense," she said. "If Carey knows there's a chance Maverick might be sold, why isn't she working with him on a daily basis? She doesn't seem to be doing anything at all."

"It does seem strange," Ty agreed. He gave a wry smile. "Then again, Carey might have ulterior motives. What if she's really staging a protest? Maybe she doesn't want Bill to sell Maverick, so she's not working with him any more."

Amy opened her eyes wide. That possibility would never have occurred to her, and she felt slightly defensive on Carey's behalf. She opened her mouth to protest, but Ty held up his hand, stalling her.

"Think about it," he went on. "Carey's the one who's supposed to be working on the healing side. If she's not handling Maverick and helping him with his trust issues, he's not going to be good around strangers. So it'll be hard to find a buyer."

Amy's face darkened. "There are always buyers," she said, shuddering at the memory of Brad's horrible truckload. "I see what you mean, though. Bill wouldn't sell a horse to just anyone," she added. "But it still doesn't make sense. Carey should want the mustang to go to a good home, if he has to be sold."

The more she thought about it, the stranger the whole situation seemed. As they rode through a hilltop clearing, Amy felt a sudden chill strike her, in spite of the warm sun. Had Carey given up on Maverick, just like everyone else?

* * *

They rode through the trees and trotted for a while when the path flattened out. It was beautiful in the forest, with the sunlight dappling the horses' coats. Brandy and Glen were well schooled and unflappable, even when birds flew out unexpectedly and squirrels chattered in the branches. They were ideal trail-ride horses, and Amy felt a growing affection for the willing chestnut beneath her. Brandy's stride was quick and sure, and she trotted forward with her ears pricked. Amy stroked the mare's neck and let her mind drift back to her first trip. When she had come this way with Huten, it had been on foot and she hadn't known where she was going. Huten had wanted Amy to be disorientated – he had wanted her to lose her bearings and then have to find her own way back. It had been one of the lessons he used to teach her to look for new ways of seeing things. Amy had been unnerved by the experience at the time, yet Huten's motives now seemed perfectly clear to her.

The path began to descend, and the village rooftops soon became visible through the trees. The horses increased their stride as the trail widened, eventually connecting with the village's main street. Amy and Ty rode carefully along the busy road, with its craft shops, food stands, and wide-eyed tourists, until they reached a quieter area at the end, where they could tether the horses in the shade.

"This is one of the places that Huten brought me to," Amy told Ty, beckoning him up a side road. "There's something you have to see."

She led him to a little craft workshop. There was a large array of handwoven baskets and mats on the ground outside, laid out as samples of products for sale. Five or six people were crouching down, turning the baskets over in their hands. Two children at the far end were arguing, both clenching the same basket with tight fingers. As she surveyed the scene, Amy frowned. This workshop had been so quiet and restful last time, virtually unnoticed by the tourists. In fact, she and Huten had been the only ones there.

She stepped into the cool interior and felt a sharp stab of relief when she saw that at least the basket maker was still there. Several people were standing around the old man as he sat weaving. A tour guide wearing a baseball cap with a bright company logo seemed to be explaining his work. The old man looked up occasionally, blinking as cameras flashed and whirred.

"You can see how long these old-fashioned methods take. It'll take him three days to finish a basket this size," the guide was saying, holding one up. "You can't find baskets like these at Target stores, folks!"

As the group around him tittered, Amy felt a lurch of disappointment. She reached out and touched Ty's arm. "Let's go!" she whispered before turning around and heading out of the door.

Ty hesitated, taking another look at the weaver's steady hands, then followed Amy back to the street. "Hey, what's the matter?" he protested. "That was interesting. I've never seen stuff like this before."

But Amy marched away from the workshop, digging her

nails into her palms. "That's not what I wanted to show you at all. It's all ruined," she said angrily. "When I came with Huten, the basket weaver was working alone, and it seemed very peaceful and reflective. Now he's being treated like an animal in a zoo. And there are tour guides who make jokes. I bet no one ever talks with the weaver and hears what he has to say about his work."

Ty spread his hands. "Amy, things change," he said. "Maybe he's happy to be showing his work to more people. Maybe he doesn't want to talk while he weaves."

Amy pursed her lips. *It's not the same*, she thought.

"It's not ruined for me, Amy," Ty persisted gently. "I thought the guy looked pretty peaceful in there, and those baskets are amazing – at least the ones I managed to see. I mean, I was only in there about thirty seconds. Talk about rude tourists." He glanced over his shoulder and grinned.

Amy forced a smile. Her frustration lingered, but she knew they should move on. "Oh, well, I guess we can head to the stream. That won't have changed, anyhow."

Brandy and Glen were already dozing, their bottom lips dangling soft and relaxed, their tails swishing away flies. Brandy snorted sleepily as Amy remounted, and Amy let her have a long rein as they walked back through the village. They were about to turn on to the path that led to the woods when something caught Amy's eye. She reined in Brandy sharply.

Ty rode up beside her. "What is it?" he queried.

"Look," said Amy in a low voice. She pointed to the cluster of buildings that formed the core of the village. One of them looked like a community centre, and in the courtyard outside sat a group of children. Sitting cross-legged in front of them, long dark hair falling on to her shoulders, was a familiar figure. Amy stared. It was Carey! She seemed to be telling some kind of story, using hand gestures to emphasize particular parts. Every so often she laughed out loud, sounding more relaxed than Amy could have imagined from her brittle behaviour back at the ranch. The children were rapt, totally absorbed in what she was saying.

"I didn't know she did that kind of stuff," commented Ty.

"Neither did I," said Amy with feeling.

Not wanting to disturb her, she nudged Brandy forward, but just as she did so, Carey looked up. Amy hesitated, then waved. Carey looked down again quickly and continued her story, making a face that drew easy laughter from the kids. Amy felt a stab of rejection. The other girl carried on with intense focus, and Amy released her reins and allowed Brandy to walk down the street.

"She could have waved back," Amy remarked to Ty as they climbed back into the woods.

"Well, I guess it was difficult. There must be a lot of pressure, being surrounded by all those kids," Ty replied reasonably.

It was a typically forgiving comment from Ty, but Amy couldn't share his open-minded judgement; she was still smarting, partly from Carey outright ignoring her and partly because she hadn't even mentioned this side of her life to Amy.

"If she's working in the village, maybe that's why she's not taking care of Maverick any more," Amy wondered aloud.

Ty looked doubtful. "I think there has to be something more," he said. "Give it time, Amy."

Amy shrugged and gave Brandy a squeeze with her calves. It was cooler among the trees, and the horses trotted briskly up the hill until they reached a fork. Amy checked the map.

"We go left here," she said over her shoulder to Ty. She glanced at him as she turned Brandy on to a trail that joined a crystal-clear trout stream. After following it for a while, they came to a small clearing where a huge flat boulder jutted out, overhanging the stream. Amy reined in the chestnut mare and swung herself out of the saddle.

"This is another of Huten's places," she said.

She gazed around her and felt the disappointment from seeing the basket weaver's shop ebb away. This was a dazzling spot, with the sunlight glinting on the gurgling water and a soft breeze rustling through the trees – and, best of all, it sparkled exactly as it had the first time. It filled Amy with the same hopeful exhilaration.

After tying up the horses' reins so that they could graze, Amy and Ty scrambled on to the rock and sat with their feet dangling over the edge.

"I followed Huten here on foot," Amy explained quietly. "We sat for a bit, then he disappeared into the woods. I couldn't see which way he'd gone, and at first I panicked. But it was all part of what he was teaching me – that you can always find your own way."

Ty smiled. "Sounds like he taught you in riddles."

Amy cocked her head to one side. "Not riddles exactly." It

was difficult to explain the subtle methods that Huten had used in his teachings. You had to experience them for yourself. She looked down into the stream and once more felt her heart clench with grief that the old man was gone.

They sat in silence for a few moments, then Ty got to his feet. Amy watched as he clambered down the side of the rock to the water and crouched down to select a handful of flat, rounded pebbles. With an expert flick of his wrist, he sent them skimming one by one over a clear stretch of water upstream. Amy watched each of them bounce three, four, five times before disappearing with a little *gloop*.

When he had thrown them all, Ty turned and looked up at her, an impish grin on his face. "I haven't done that since I was about ten," he said, pulling himself back on to the rock.

Amy smiled, and their eyes met. Ty reached for her hand.

"Thank you for bringing me here," he said softly. "I know it's not the same for you without Huten, but I can tell it's a special place." He drew closer to Amy and put his arm around her.

Amy regretted any doubts she'd ever had about bringing Ty along. He had shown nothing but patience since arriving at Ten Beeches. She was spoiling things by resenting his presence and trying to cling to her own memories. She thought of Carey's dismissive behaviour and was relieved that he was there to support her. Once again, she remembered Lou's words about how grateful she might be to have Ty along with her and recognized that her sister had been right.

She looked down at the glinting stream once more and listened to the birds calling, the branches swaying, and the tiny munching sounds of the horses nibbling at leaves. It was so serene;one of the loveliest places she had ever shared with Ty. She moved closer to him so that their cheeks were nearly brushing and let herself take in the moment and the surroundings.

She didn't know how long they sat there. They only stirred when a woodpecker called loudly nearby, its laughing voice echoing through the forest.

"We'd better get back," said Amy.

She didn't need to look at the map – she could remember the way back as clearly as if she had walked it yesterday. They caught the horses and remounted. Ty patted Glen as he took up the reins and set off down the path, but Amy paused and looked back at the spot where Huten had left her the first time she had visited the stream. A lump rose in her throat as she bade her old friend her own heartfelt farewell.

Goodbye, Huten, she thought. Then she gathered up Brandy's reins and followed Ty down the path.

Chapter Six

As they rode back towards Ten Beeches, Ty raised the subject of Carey again. "Maybe you need to spend some time with her, to get to the bottom of what's going on," he said. "Something tells me she's not going to open up with me here. If she's around tomorrow, I'll stay out of the way. I'll help Bill in the yard or go on one of the trail rides."

"I guess that makes sense," Amy agreed. "If you're sure you don't mind." She glanced across at him, wondering if he was at all affected by Carey's unwelcoming attitude. If he was, he was certainly putting on a brave face. He only seemed to be thinking of Carey and what she was going through, and that was Amy's primary concern, too. And then there was Maverick.

Ty smiled. "This trail ride has already made the whole trip worthwhile, as far as I'm concerned. It's been good to take it all in and see it through your eyes."

They rode back into the yard to find that Bill had already returned with his group of tourists. Amy guessed that she and Ty had avoided passing them on the trail by turning off and going to the stream. Some of the group were standing around chatting, while others were drifting towards their cars. Carey was also back from the village and was helping Bill and Aiden untack the horses and take them to their stalls. Amy smiled at her awkwardly as she unbuckled Brandy's girth, and Carey offered a self-conscious smile in return.

Amy gave Brandy a good rubdown, then made a point of looking for her friend in the other stalls, hoping they'd have an opportunity to talk. But the only people she found were Aiden and Bill.

"Have you seen Carey?" Amy asked Bill.

"You just missed her. She went back into town with her mother," he told her. "They'll be back before supper."

"Oh, OK," said Amy, disappointed. "I guess I'll see her later. Do you know if she'll be around tomorrow?"

"She should be," Bill assured her, giving a thoughtful nod.

"OK, thanks," said Amy, flashing him a smile. She wandered off to find Ty in Rugged Glen's stall, where he was combing burrs and bits of twig from the grey horse's tail. She immediately launched into the latest on the Carey front, telling him about Carey's most recent disappearing act. "Why did she want me to come if she's going to avoid me all week?"

Ty teased out a thorny twig with his fingers. "Hey," he said, "don't think like that. We've only been here a day. I'm sure you'll be able to talk to her tomorrow, or even later on tonight."

"I guess." Amy reached up and ran her fingers through the gelding's forelock. Carey sure wasn't making things easy for her, but Ty was right. An opportunity would arise before long.

But after supper that evening, Bill and Barbara suggested a game of cards, and Amy felt it would be rude to drag Carey off for a talk on their own. In any case, it seemed to be the last thing Carey wanted. After a few rounds of reluctant rummy, she excused herself for the night. As the other girl left the room, Amy looked across at Ty and gave a resigned shrug. There was no point in pursuing her if she was determined not to talk. Perhaps Amy just had to make herself available and let Carey come to her in her own time.

The next morning, Amy joined Ty in the yard, where Bill and Aiden were busy mucking out the stalls. "I wonder how Maverick's doing today?" she mused, and they wandered over to his stall together.

The little horse rolled his eyes when he saw them, but when Ty held out a handful of horse cookies, he stepped forward and lipped them from his palm.

"That's it," Ty murmured, letting himself into the stall. "Don't be afraid. I'm just coming to say hello."

Maverick backed off a step or two, then stopped. At first, the horse's eyes rolled with uncertainty, but Amy could see recognition there, too. Ty reached forward and stroked his neck.

"I think he's taken to you," said Amy. "Maybe Bill would let you work with him today."

"What's that?" asked Bill's voice. He came and stood next to Amy. "Did I hear my name? Are you talking about me?"

Amy and Ty laughed when they realized Bill was trying to be funny. "We were just thinking that Maverick's looking a bit happier today," she explained. "He seems to like Ty."

Bill peered into the stall, and Amy caught his look of surprise. Ty was massaging the horse's back in little T-touch circles while Maverick stood still, his eyelids drooping.

"Well, that's a piece of good news," said Bill. "Actually, it's good timing, too. There's a prospective buyer coming to see him tomorrow, so he could do with some handling – even riding, if you think you could manage it."

Amy looked at Ty. She was thrilled that Bill trusted him enough already to work with Maverick, but she'd let Ty decide how involved he wanted to get with the troubled horse.

"I'd love to," Ty said. "Any chance of bringing him out on the trails with you? Amy wants to stay here for the day, and I don't think it would be a good idea to ride him out on my own."

"No, I wouldn't let you," agreed Bill. "A trail ride sounds like a good plan. I'm taking a group out at ten – just a couple of locals. They know horses pretty well, so they won't be turned off if he acts up."

With Ty's morning planned out, Amy went inside, wondering when Carey would appear. It was difficult to work out what her routine was – or if she even had one. The family didn't gather for breakfast; the only time that everyone seemed to be together was at dinnertime. All Amy had to go on was Bill's assurance that Carey would be at Ten Beeches today.

But other than Barbara, the cabin seemed deserted. Thinking that Carey might get up later than everyone else, Amy decided to stay in the main room for a while and take a look through some of Huten's old books. She found the one that her mother had borrowed from him, *Hearing the Silence*. It was an old hardback with faded edges, containing stories, poetry and songs from the Native American tradition. Amy read the inscription he had written for Marion: "When this book no longer holds any answers, the time is right." She sighed. Amy knew that Marion had planned on returning to Ten Beeches, just as Amy was doing now. But that time had never come.

Putting the book down, Amy went to the kitchen. Barbara was running her finger along the lines of a recipe, and looked up when she heard Amy come in.

"Can I help with anything?" Amy asked. "I'm trying to make myself feel useful."

Barbara snapped the book shut and smiled. "I'm sure I could find something for you to do. Are you handy with a potato peeler?" She got a bag of potatoes and tipped some into the sink. "The peeler's in the drawer," she said.

Amy covered the potatoes with warm water and began to scrape at the muddy skins.

"Not out with the horses today?" Barbara asked, giving Amy a curious look.

"Well, to be honest, I was hoping I'd run into Carey," Amy confessed as she struggled with the peeler, which seemed a little dull. "She's not out in the yard, so I thought she had to be here somewhere."

"Ah," said Barbara. "You know, Amy, Carey's a lot like her grandfather. You have to look sideways to catch her. It's no use approaching her head-on."

Amy frowned, wondering what Barbara meant. She was beginning to get a strange sense of déjà vu, as though her first visit was repeating itself. She had felt as lost and bewildered then as she did now, with the whole family seeming to be aware of secrets and hidden meanings that lay beyond her understanding.

She tried to find a response.

"I know what you mean about them being alike," she said, thinking it was a lame reply. "Carey must really miss him."

Barbara nodded. "We all do," she said. "But it was his time to go. He was ready."

Amy looked at Barbara's calm features and frowned. This family's grief was so different from her own. She had never been able to feel that her mother was ready to go.

"It doesn't mean we miss him any less," Barbara went on softly, as if she could read Amy's thoughts.

Amy forced a smile and turned back to the sink. She heard Barbara sigh. "Carey's glad you've come, even if you can't see it right now," said the older woman.

Are you sure? thought Amy, rinsing off one of the potatoes. *Is it that I can't see it or that she isn't showing it?* For a moment, she wondered if Barbara really had any idea what was going on in Carey's mind. Carey seemed so unhappy and estranged from her family. Just because they were mother and daughter, it didn't necessarily mean that they understood each other.

Amy knew there was only one way to find out what was going on. She *had* to speak to Carey. She finished the potatoes and covered them in water, then went outside with the peelings and threw them on to the compost pile. Barbara had no other chores for her, so Amy headed back to the yard. Her only thought was that Carey was out in the woods. She wondered if it would be worth trying to find her.

Ty and Bill had already gone, and Amy peered into the stalls to see which horses had been left behind. She recognized

Sandy, the mare that Carey had ridden into the woods last time she'd visited. *Looks like Brandy's sister*, she was thinking to herself when the slam of a stall door made her jump. She wheeled round.

Carey was marching towards her, her face like thunder. "They took Maverick! No one rides Maverick besides me. What kind of crazy idea was that?"

Amy stared at her, speechless, as Carey crossed her arms and glared at her. "I don't suppose you and your *boyfriend* have anything to do with this, do you?"

The words hung in the air and Amy felt herself blush. On the one hand, she felt guilty, because it *was* Ty who had taken Maverick out. On the other, Carey's reaction was all out of proportion, and Amy felt her own anger rising. "We just wanted to help," she said defensively.

"Help!" Carey's voice rose.

"Look," said Amy, trying to stay calm. "When we spoke on the phone, you asked me to come and see you, and you said something about Maverick. Ty's worked with plenty of horses like him before, so there won't be a prob—"

"Is Maverick all you can think about?" Carey's face was tight and cold.

Amy felt baffled. What did Carey *want* her to think about? "He's one unhappy horse, Carey," she said. "Of course I care about that. And Ty knows what he's doing, believe it or not."

Carey's eyes flashed. "Oh, you and Ty have it all figured out, don't you?" she snapped.

"No!" said Amy, exasperated. "I just happen to work with

71

difficult horses, and so does Ty. Remember?"

Carey fell silent, and Amy tried to gather her thoughts. *This isn't about you*, she told herself. *Try to see beyond it.* "Your dad told us that someone's coming to see Maverick tomorrow," she said tentatively. "I don't know what's going on, but I guess you're not too happy about selling him yet. Is that the problem?"

Carey didn't seem to hear her. "You can tell Ty I don't need his help," she spat angrily. "I didn't ask for it. I don't even know why he's here."

Amy took a step back, stung. It was one thing to guess why Carey was being so unwelcoming and another to hear it out loud. "Well, I'm glad he's here," she said, before she could stop herself. "You haven't exactly been the best company since we arrived."

Carey's face blanched, and Amy bit her lip. She could guess how much pain lay behind her friend's behaviour, and she didn't want to make things worse. She took a deep breath. "Carey, I know how difficult things must be for you right now. But whatever you think, I *do* want to help, if you'll let me."

Carey looked at Amy for a moment, and Amy held her gaze. It suddenly occurred to her that Carey was a little like an ungentled horse – wild and mistrustful, keeping her distance even though deep down she might be longing to make contact.

"Right now, you can help by leaving me alone," Carey said abruptly, startling Amy out of her sympathetic thoughts. "I'm going for a ride." She turned on her heel and strode away.

Amy hesitated, then marched after her. "I'm coming

with you," she announced.

Carey stopped and glared at her, her eyes bright with frustration.

"I'm your guest," Amy pointed out. "You can't just leave me here."

Carey pursed her lips and looked away. Then she started striding to the tack room. "You can ride Sandy," she called in an ungracious tone over her shoulder.

It was hardly a reconciliation, but it was a start. Feeling relieved, Amy followed her and looked for Sandy's tack. Without saying any more, she hoisted the saddle on to her arm and went back outside. The two girls tacked up in silence.

To Amy's secret delight, she saw that Carey was going to ride Albatross. She hadn't seen much of the lovely paint horse since her arrival. She mounted Sandy and followed Carey out of the yard.

They took a path that skirted the woods and walked in single file for a while. Amy watched the other girl ride, thinking that, in the saddle, Carey looked more like Huten than ever. It was a shame that she didn't seem to have her grandfather's easy patience right now. Amy wondered if Huten had always been so measured and wise. Perhaps he hadn't. Sure, he was a natural with horses, but if he had been anything like his granddaughter, it might have taken him a long time to find himself. He might have had to learn how to see life in his own special way. Amy found the thought oddly reassuring.

Carey soon pushed Albatross into a trot, and Amy quickly asked Sandy to follow. Like the mare she had taken out yesterday, Sandy was a lovely, eager ride. If anything, her stride was even smoother than Brandy's, and Amy allowed herself to relax for a while to enjoy the even rhythm. Then, when the path widened, she gritted her teeth and pushed the mare forward to ride alongside Albatross.

"Seeing you on Albatross reminds me of Huten," she began, hoping she wouldn't somehow offend Carey. "I can still remember watching him ride bareback around the training ring. It was really something."

Carey gave a shrug. "Everyone says that," she said.

"Well, it's true," said Amy, but Carey had already turned Albatross on to a narrow uphill path. Frustrated, Amy fell in behind her on Sandy, and they trotted between the trees on a winding trail that took them deeper into the mountains. When they reached the top of an incline, Carey reined Albatross in and looked out over the tops of the trees. The folds of the mountains rose and fell away from them as far as Amy could see, thickly covered with dark green pine trees that were sliced through here and there by plunging silver streams.

She drew up alongside Carey and decided to try another tack. "I was surprised to see you down in the village," she said. "How long have you been working there?"

Carey looked at her sharply. "I'm not working there," she said. "The village elders who work at the community centre asked me to do a storytelling hour for the kids now and then. That's all."

"Well, it looked impressive," Amy told her. "Those kids couldn't get enough of you."

Carey gave one of her derisive snorts and said nothing.

"Listen," said Amy. "I'm sorry about what I said earlier. I know it's tough for you right now. You must be really missing him – Huten, I mean."

Carey reached down to adjust one of her stirrup leathers, and her hair fell forward so Amy couldn't see her face. "Of course I miss Huten," she said.

"Well, I'm sorry," repeated Amy awkwardly. "Things must be really different around here without him."

Carey looked straight at her. "You don't know how different," she said. "And the sooner I leave, the better."

Chapter Seven

"Leave?" Amy echoed in disbelief. She stared at Carey. "But I thought you'd decided to stay! What about everything we talked about last time? You belong here!"

It had never occurred to her that Carey might abandon Huten's work altogether now that he wasn't around. Sure, Amy knew Carey had considered moving away when Huten was still alive, but she had come to realize that her bonds with Huten and Ocanumba were stronger than she'd thought. How could she betray his memory and go back on that now? And what about Maverick? Where did he fit in?

Amy drew a deep breath. "I don't get it," she said.

Carey raised her eyebrows. "I can see that."

She clicked her tongue and rode on, guiding Albatross along a path that Amy thought she recognized. They had joined a track that led to Carey's favourite place in the forest, a cavern by a tumbling waterfall. Amy followed her in silence, wondering what on earth she could say next.

They reached a little clearing near the falls. Carey dismounted and tied Albatross's reins around his neck as Amy swung herself out of Sandy's saddle. Here, Carey already seemed more relaxed, and she even smiled as she beckoned Amy forward. "Remember coming here last time?" she asked.

Amy nodded, still shaken by Carey's words. "How could I forget?"

Leaving the horses to graze in the clearing, the two girls walked through a big cleft in the rock and along a slippery path that led down towards the river. The waterfall soon came into sight, a gushing torrent that poured from a rocky ledge high among the trees on the mountainside. It was breathtaking.

Amy clambered towards the water until she could feel the cool spray on her face. She sat down on a boulder and closed her eyes, letting her senses fill with the roar of the cascade and the gentle mist on her skin. This was another amazing place, wild and isolated, so different from the rolling hills around Heartland. And then she remembered that it was coming here that had convinced her of Carey's bond with Ocanumba last time. Was Carey really so sure she was making the right decision? She opened her eyes and looked around.

There was no sign of Carey. Amy guessed that she had gone to the huge cavern close to the waterfall that held significance for her ancestors. There was a fissure at the top of the cave that let in a shaft of daylight. Amy remembered that it was known as One Eye. She pushed herself to her feet and made her way into the cave.

She stood at the entrance and peered inside. It took a few moments for her eyes to adjust, but then she saw Carey sitting cross-legged, leaning against the wall.

Amy stepped inside. "Mind if I join you?"

Carey gave a brief smile, shaking her head, and Amy sat down next to her friend on the sandy floor. The light from One Eye created a tiny pool of flickering brightness, and Amy stared at it, fascinated.

"How can you think of leaving this incredible place?" she blurted out impulsively, then wished she hadn't. Carey was still so selective about the barriers she would let down, and Amy didn't want to alienate her again.

But Carey just leaned forward and picked up a handful of sand. "I'm not saying I won't miss it," she said, pouring the sand from one hand to the other. "It's just not the only special place in the world, that's all."

"Maybe," said Amy. She hesitated. "But others might not be easy to find."

"That's not the point. The searching is what counts." Carey lifted her eyes and looked curiously at Amy. "Haven't you ever thought about leaving Heartland? Do you really think you'll stay there for the rest of your life?"

Amy felt uneasy. Of course, she'd have to make decisions about her own future before long; she was approaching the end of high school, and things were bound to change after that. But she didn't want to think about it yet. "Heartland's my home," she said. "All the people I love are there – Lou, Ty, Grandpa."

Carey smiled, a strange, gentle smile tinged with sadness. "Just because you love a place or a person, it doesn't mean you can't leave them."

Amy's heart beat faster. *That can't be true*, she wanted to protest – yet she knew that it was. Life at Heartland was full of connections that were forged, only to be broken when horses and people moved on. But it didn't apply to the ones who really mattered, did it? She searched for a response. "So what about Maverick?" she challenged. "Is that why you've given up on him?"

Carey's face tightened. "Who says I've given up on him?"

An edge of anger had returned to her voice, and Amy wished she'd chosen her words more carefully. "Well, that's the way it looks to me," she said uncertainly.

Carey gave her a long, hard stare before allowing her features to soften once more. "Then you'd be wrong," she said. She threw the handful of sand on to the ground, brushed her hands together and scrambled to her feet.

Back in the bright sunlight, they caught the horses and unknotted their reins. Amy managed to convince Sandy that she'd had enough grass and was about to lift her foot to the stirrup when Carey led Albatross over.

"Here. Take Albatross," she said, handing Amy the reins. "I know you'd like to ride him."

Amy was taken aback. "Are you sure?"

"Don't worry. Albatross goes for anyone. That's the way Huten trained him. He's an angel."

"Well, OK. Thanks." Amy hesitated, then swung herself into the paint horse's saddle, an old, ornate Western one, the leather soft and supple. Amy imagined the care and attention it had received from Huten and almost felt as though she were sitting on something sacred. But Carey seemed to think it was perfectly normal for someone else to ride her grandfather's horse, and watching her friend swing herself on to Sandy's back, Amy felt confused. Again, she thought about how this family seemed to have such a different approach to grief. The grief was there – there was no doubt about that. But Amy wasn't sure that she could have been so unemotional about Pegasus after her mother's death. After all, she reminded herself grimly, she was finding it hard enough to share Spindle's training with Joni. *Take it as a compliment*, she thought as they started down the trail once more. Somehow, she needed to convince herself that it was OK to enjoy riding Huten's horse.

It was not long before Amy's cares were forgotten. Albatross was a joy to ride. His stride was fluid and comfortable, but more than that, he responded to the gentlest aids and the slightest shift in Amy's weight. Amy watched his flicking ears, sensing that he was anticipating her every command.

"We'll take a route where we can canter," Carey called over her shoulder, and Amy grinned. Cantering on Albatross would be amazing, and she leaned forward to stroke his neck.

The trail widened and Carey set off at a fast pace, giving Sandy her head. Amy waited a second or two, then allowed Albatross to follow. With a snort of excitement, the paint horse leaped forward, his long, powerful strides devouring the ground. Amy felt the wind on her face and laughed out loud, relishing the kaleidoscope of forest colours that blurred around her.

The canter came to an end all too soon. Carey and Sandy returned to a trot, then a walk. Amy reined in Albatross, praising him and clapping his neck. "That was fantastic," she enthused. "He's such an amazing horse."

Carey grinned at her. "Thought you might enjoy it," she said. "Albatross makes everyone feel special."

She turned Sandy down a narrow path, and Amy fell in

behind her once more, still a little breathless. Albatross was a dream horse, trained to perfection. But as they followed the winding path down towards Ten Beeches, she thought about what Carey had just said. Albatross wasn't just well trained. It was much more than that. She remembered Huten telling her that he had been a rogue horse, one that other people had given up on because of his defensive, aggressive behaviour. But with Huten's care and direction, he had learned to accept people, and now he gave himself to his rider with willing, open pleasure. It was as though Huten's generous spirit lived on in the horse. Amy *did* feel special.

An image of Spindleberry suddenly popped into Amy's mind. As difficult as it was to admit, she knew that she'd wanted to do all the yearling's training herself – part of her wanted him to feel that special bond with her and no one else. Yet deep down, she knew that nothing would make her happier than for the yearling to turn out like Albatross. Encouraging that to happen would be easier said than done, however. She wondered how Joni was getting along with him and decided to phone Heartland when they got back to Ten Beeches.

Amy patted the paint horse, thinking about Carey. Her friend clearly understood Huten's wisdom, at least in relation to Albatross, and was willing to pass it on by sharing the wonderful horse. So what about Maverick? Back at the cave, Carey had said that she hadn't given up on him. But if that was the case, why wasn't she working with him more – and why was he still such a handful? Nothing was adding up, and Amy knew there were still a lot more answers to find.

* * *

The yard was quiet when they got back, deserted apart from a few horses dozing, their heads over their half-doors.

Amy dismounted and went round to Albatross's head. "Thank you," she murmured, kissing his nose. "Carey's right. You're an angel."

As she reached up to undo his throat latch, she heard the sound of horses approaching the yard. Bill rode in at the head of the group. The two trail riders followed close after him, and Amy looked anxiously for Ty, hoping that Maverick hadn't been too much of a problem. There was a pause, then Ty rode slowly into the yard with Maverick on a long rein. Amy felt relieved. The mustang looked calm and well exercised; there hadn't been a disaster, at least.

But to Amy's surprise, Carey led Sandy over, her face dark with fury. "Unsaddle her for me, will you?" she said abruptly, handing Amy the reins. With her shoulders back and chin raised in determination, she marched across the yard to Ty, who was just dismounting.

"I'll take him now," she snapped, snatching Maverick's reins. "What did you think you were doing? Do you have any idea how stupid it was to take him out on a trail ride?"

"Maverick's fine," Ty said calmly, remaining unruffled despite Carey's harsh words. "He's not wound up at all. In fact—"

"Fine?" retorted Carey. "You're lucky you didn't break your neck. The sooner everyone realizes that I'm the only one who can ride him the better."

Abruptly turning away from Ty, she hurried Maverick

towards his stall. But from the other side of the yard, Amy could see her expression clearly. Carey was almost in tears, and as she briefly cradled the mustang's head, Amy suddenly saw the truth. Carey didn't *want* Maverick to work well with anyone else! She loved him too much, too fiercely. She wanted the mustang to be hers – and hers alone.

Chapter Eight

Ty shrugged and walked over to Amy. She felt awful, as though she was somehow responsible for Carey's outburst. "Are you OK?" she asked.

Ty nodded, his mouth in a tight line. "She'll get over it," he said. He pointed to the horses Amy was holding. "Let me take one of these two. Looks like you've got your hands full."

Amy handed him Sandy's reins. "So how was Maverick out on the trails?" she asked in a low voice as they unsaddled the horses.

"Well, he wasn't what I'd call an easy ride," Ty admitted. "He napped and pulled a lot at first, spooked at shadows, that sort of thing. He gradually eased up, but I had to keep my distance from the other horses – they seemed to bother him more than anything."

"That makes sense," said Amy. "I guess he'll never completely forget being bullied."

"No," agreed Ty. "And I guess if Carey's the only one who rides him, he feels pretty vulnerable when she's not around."

As Amy lifted the saddle off Albatross's back and hoisted it on to her arm, she realized that Ty had hit the nail on the head. Huten had fallen ill, and Carey had kept Maverick all to herself. She had helped the horse recover from a significant trauma and had gained his total trust. It must have seemed very special, for a while. But now that she was going to leave, her exclusive understanding of him had suddenly become a problem.

* * *

Amy and Ty took the tack indoors, then went back out to settle the horses and give them a quick rubdown. Once Albatross was pulling at his hay net, Amy looked around the yard. The trail riders had long since left, and there was no sign of Bill or Aiden. She hesitated as she walked by Maverick's stall, wondering if Carey was still there with him. On reflection, she decided to leave her alone.

As Ty came out of Sandy's stall, Amy remembered that she'd planned on calling Heartland. "I'm just going to give Lou a quick call on my cell," she told him, fishing the phone from her pocket. "It would be good to know how Joni's getting along."

"Sure," said Ty. He raised an eyebrow. "Less eventfully than we are, I hope."

Amy smiled wryly in agreement and punched in the number. After a few rings, Lou answered.

"Hi, Lou," said Amy. "It's me. How's everything going?"

"Amy! Good to hear from you. We're all fine. How are you and Ty?"

"Oh, we're OK," said Amy. "It's so pretty here. You were right, though. Things are different without Huten."

"I thought they might be," Lou responded. "But no major problems, I hope?"

"Nothing we can't handle," said Amy, smiling at Ty. "Actually, I was wondering how Joni's doing, with all the horses and — and Spindle."

"The horses are all fine. Joni's on top of everything," Lou

85

assured her. "D'you want me to call her to the phone? She can tell you more specifics."

Amy hesitated. She was dying to know what Spindle had been up to and what Joni might have taught him, but something made her hold back. Whatever the stable girl was doing, Amy knew she was powerless to interfere, and in some ways it was easier not to know what the eager yearling was taking on without her there. "No. No, that's OK. As long as things are under control."

"Yes, you enjoy the rest of the week," said Lou. "If anything goes wrong you'll be the first to know, don't worry."

"Thanks, Lou." Amy said goodbye and clicked off the phone. The image of Spindleberry's face flashed before her, but she pushed it away. She was here to concentrate on Carey and Maverick, and that was what she was going to do.

She looked at Ty, suddenly realizing how hungry she was. "Should we go in?" she asked. "We might be able to find some lunch."

"Sure. I just hope Carey's cooled down," said Ty. "Any more of those explosions would kill my appetite."

"I'm so sorry, Ty," consoled Amy.

"You're not responsible for what she says, remember?"

"I know. I just feel bad," said Amy as they headed for the cabin.

They took off their boots and went inside. They were greeted by the delicious aroma of fresh coffee and found Bill, Aiden and Barbara in the kitchen. It looked as though Barbara had made a mountain of sandwiches.

"Come on in and help yourselves," Barbara said brightly, handing them each a plate. "I thought you'd all be in need of a snack. Did you have a good ride?"

"Um, great, thank you," said Amy as she and Ty sat down. She shot a look at Bill, who was pouring the coffee. Amy knew he must have seen Carey's outburst in the yard, but it was difficult to read his expression. How did Bill and Barbara feel about Carey's decision to leave, she wondered. She reached for a ham and cheese sandwich and was taking a bite when Carey came in.

"Hi, honey," Barbara greeted her.

Carey's face was still closed and angry. She took the plate that her mother offered but didn't sit down. She selected two sandwiches and began to eat them standing up, by the kitchen door. No one commented. Amy finished her sandwich and started on another.

"There was a phone call from Jason Montague this morning," said Barbara, putting a plateful of cookies on the table, "confirming that he's coming to see Maverick tomorrow at twelve. That's still OK, isn't it?"

She might as well have dropped a bomb on the kitchen. The atmosphere instantly became electric. Even Bill looked uneasy, but he shrugged and said, "Well, he didn't go too badly for Ty today. We'll need to explain his background. Hopefully this guy will be sympathetic."

Amy turned to see Carey cough, choking on her sandwich. Then, her eyes smouldering with disgust, Carey banged her plate down on the kitchen worktop. "I don't know how you can think of selling him," she said to her father, her voice shaking.

"He'll hate it so much. Don't you remember what we rescued him from? This is his home. Huten would never have sold him."

Bill wearily passed a hand across his face, and Amy guessed that they had been over this many times before. "Look," he said, "we can't use Maverick for trail rides. If we could, then of course we would. You know that, Carey."

"Maverick was never supposed to be ridden by schoolkids on vacation," she protested. "Do you think Huten would have been happy with that? We never used to turn rescued horses into trail hacks."

Carey was clearly being unfair. Amy thought of Sandy, Brandy and Rugged Glen – all so much more than "trail hacks" – and saw anger spring into Bill's eyes, but he held his tongue and said nothing. It was Barbara who spoke instead. "Then we can't afford to keep him," she said. "There'll be no role for him here. If you were going to stay, honey, it might be different."

Amy looked at her friend and felt a rush of sympathy. She was beginning to see just how she felt. Huten's healing work at Ten Beeches was coming to an end, and there was a part of Carey that desperately wanted to preserve his legacy. But how could she, when she herself had decided to leave Ocanumba?

Carey glared at her parents before storming out of the kitchen. At the end of the cabin, Amy heard the muffled sound of her bedroom door slamming shut. She realized she'd been holding her breath and let it out slowly, raising her eyebrows at Ty. He reached for her hand and squeezed it under the table.

An uncomfortable silence fell on the kitchen. Aiden muttered a quick thank you for the lunch and slipped outside.

Amy found she couldn't eat any more and put her sandwich back on her plate.

"Can we help you clean up?" she asked Barbara.

"No, no," said Barbara. She gave a forced smile. "Why don't you two head out? It's a beautiful day."

Amy and Ty didn't need any more encouragement. They got up and left Bill and Barbara sitting together at the table. It clearly wasn't the time to sit around making polite small talk.

It was a relief to get out of the strained family atmosphere and into the warm afternoon sunshine. "Poor Carey," murmured Amy as they wandered down towards the pasture.

Ty frowned. "I have more sympathy for Maverick, actually," he said. "And Bill and Barbara. Carey seems to be going out of her way to make things difficult for everyone."

"I can see what you mean," Amy agreed. "But Carey really loves that horse, you know."

"She has a funny way of showing it." Ty's face was clouded. "He needs her around to feel safe. Now he's going to be sold, and she isn't doing anything to make it easier for him. Do you really think that's love, Amy?"

Amy fell silent, thinking of her ride into the forest with Carey and what the other girl had told her. Ty's words were fair enough. Huten would have handled the half mustang very differently – Albatross was proof enough of that. But Amy was sure that Carey never meant Maverick to be unhappy. She simply didn't want to let him go, not just because she loved him but because he was the last horse that she and Huten had worked with together. She thought of Carey's words: *Huten would never have sold him.* Letting go of Maverick meant saying goodbye to her grandfather, and however much Carey needed to do that, it was still terribly painful.

"She just can't win," Amy said slowly. "Carey wants to leave Ten Beeches, Ty. That's what she told me today. She's always wanted to find out what the world beyond Ocanumba has to offer. But she loves Maverick and wants to keep him here as a reminder of Huten. Once Maverick's gone, that's it. No more rescue horses."

"Well, I guess," said Ty, sounding more sympathetic. "But there's still Albatross."

"Albatross is a perfect gentleman," said Amy. "I'm sure Bill will use him on the trails. Albatross doesn't *need* Carey in the way that Maverick does."

They reached the paddock gate. Two of the trail horses, Mushroom and Ruby, ambled over to nose around for treats, then wandered off and continued their grazing.

"Well, you seem to understand Carey better than anyone else," said Ty. "I know it must be tough for her, but she seems to want everything her own way. I guess she wants Bill and Barbara to keep Maverick so that he's here when she visits. That's not fair to them, or to Maverick." He shook his head. "I just hate to see a horse battling like that. I don't care what Carey says, I'm going to help him get through tomorrow."

Amy nodded. "Sure," she said quietly. "I know what you're saying, and you're right. But I still feel for Carey. She's got herself into an impossible situation. I think she needs someone to help her, too."

* * *

Dinner was subdued. Carey didn't make an appearance, and Amy wondered if she should go and find her. She decided against it. She knew the other girl well enough to understand that she needed her own space at times.

It was a relief when the evening was over. Bill and Barbara seemed happy to let Ty and Amy have an early night. Amy got into bed and lay awake, her mind churning. She thought of riding Albatross – being carried through the forest with such power and grace – and then her thoughts drifted to Carey and her decision to leave Ten Beeches. With all the fuss about Maverick, it was easy to forget what that must mean. Her plans were causing an awful lot of upheaval – not only for the people and horses around her, but for Carey herself. How could her friend be so sure it was the right thing to do? Amy thought of the words that had disturbed her so much: *Just because you love a place or a person, it doesn't mean you can't leave them.* They were brave words, and Amy respected Carey for that. But would her friend really follow through with her decision? If she did, she deserved all the support she could get.

In the morning, Amy and Ty made themselves toast in the kitchen. As they washed it down with orange juice from the fridge, Carey came through wearing a denim skirt and sandals. Amy's first thought was that she wasn't dressed for barn work, and Carey acted like the horses were the furthest thing from her mind.

"See you later," she said briefly and headed out.

Amy and Ty watched her go. "I guess the last thing she wants is to be around when that buyer comes," Amy commented, taking a last bite of toast.

Ty shook his head. "I don't really see why," he said. "I think I'd be more concerned about making sure my horse went to a good home. She's acting like she doesn't care at all."

Amy could see his point. But she could still picture Carey's expression the day before, leading Maverick across the yard after she had taken him away from Ty. She knew that the other girl felt far more pain than she ever let on.

Amy and Ty washed their dishes and went outside. They found Aiden mucking out and offered to help. "You'll have to share the wheelbarrow," he told them, handing them each a fork. "We've only got two."

"That's OK," said Amy. "It'll be fun."

It felt good to be doing something useful, and the three of them soon had the job finished. As they gave the forks back to Aiden, Bill walked across the yard with a sack of grain balanced on his shoulder and stopped when he saw them.

"Morning," he said. "Thanks for helping out. Aiden's going out on the trails with a big group later, if you'd like to go with him."

"Actually, we were wondering if you'd like some help with Maverick," said Ty. "You know, when the buyer comes. I think I can help keep him calm."

Bill looked grateful. "Well, thank you. I'm sorry you two had to get dragged into all this. You must think it's awful mean, selling him, but sometimes there's not much choice."

"We understand," said Amy.

"Horses aren't cheap to keep," Ty offered, trying to show his support.

Bill looked from Amy to Ty and back again. He seemed older than Amy had remembered, and she suddenly saw lines of grief etched in his patient features. Losing Huten had affected everyone in their own way.

"Carey's a caged bird here," he said, his voice cracking. "Now that Huten's gone, she needs to spread her wings. We know that. We just wish we could make it easier for her." He gave a knowing smile and shook his head. "Or that she'd make it easier for herself."

He winched the bag of grain more firmly on to his shoulder and headed for the feed room. Amy and Ty got a grooming kit and went to Maverick's stall. To Ty's obvious delight, the little half mustang seemed pleased to see him. He pricked his ears as they entered and butted Ty with his muzzle.

"Hello, boy," he said. "Glad to see you're having a good morning."

Ty set to work with the body brush while Amy gently teased out the knots in Maverick's mane. Now that he had accepted their presence, Maverick seemed to welcome the attention. Amy was sure that much of his problem stemmed from having so little exposure to a variety of people. It was clear that Carey had built up his confidence a great deal; he now seemed a very different horse than the one that Amy had seen when she first visited. But Maverick still had a long way to go.

"I'll give him a T-touch session when we've finished," said Amy. "Unless you'd like to?"

"I think you should," said Ty. "He began to trust me yesterday, on the trail ride. The more people he starts to bond with the better."

Amy met his eyes and smiled. Even here in Ocanumba, she and Ty made the perfect team for handling troubled horses.

Jason Montague arrived on time in a muddy four-wheel-drive utility vehicle. For some reason, Amy had expected someone older, but Jason was in his early twenties – around Lou's age. He strode breezily into the yard swinging a baseball cap in one hand, and Amy's heart sank. He didn't look like the sort of person who would know how to deal with a nervous horse, and she shot an anxious glance at Ty.

"So where's the little beauty?" asked Jason, shaking hands with Bill. He grinned cheerily at Ty and Amy. "I'm looking forward to this. My dad's old horse is a real character, but he won't make it past the next road test. You know, the brakes still work but you can't get him out of first gear."

Amy smiled in spite of herself. Jason was good-humoured, at least. She listened as he explained that he needed a horse to ride around his father's cattle ranch and had been hoping to find one with mustang blood.

"Well, Maverick could be what you're looking for," said Bill, walking towards his stall. "But as I told you on the phone, he's nervous. He's used to one rider – my daughter – and he can be difficult with anyone else. He'll need careful handling."

Amy watched Jason's expression. He looked at Bill closely as he spoke and then stopped a few feet from the stall, leaning forward to peer in.

"That's OK," he said. "I could have got a wild one, but my old man talked me out of it. Said I'd be better off finding one with some training, and I guess he's right. But I wouldn't mind taking on a tricky one."

"Maverick's not what I'd call really tricky," Ty put in. "I rode him out yesterday. What he's really about is a lack of confidence. He needs an owner he can trust."

Jason turned to look at Ty and seemed to appraise him in a man-to-man kind of way. "I guess what you're trying to say is, I won't get anywhere by fighting him," he said as Bill led Maverick out of his stall.

"Got it," Ty agreed with a smile.

Amy felt a surge of relief. However macho Jason seemed on the outside, he seemed to have plenty of common sense – and, more importantly, he understood that horses responded best to trust and gentleness.

Out in the yard, Bill was having his usual battle of wills with Maverick. "Come on, boy," he urged the mustang as Maverick showed the whites of his eyes and planted his hooves, refusing to move.

Ty offered to help, and Bill handed him the lead rope. With a little encouragement, Ty got the little horse to walk up and down, then trot the length of the yard. When Jason had scrutinized him from all angles, he stepped forward to pat the mustang on the neck.

Instantly, Maverick shot backward, almost crashing into Bill.

"Hey, hey, steady," Ty soothed him. "It's OK. Easy now."

Jason looked surprised and slightly mortified. "He sure is jumpy," he said. "How about I try that again?"

He stepped forward again, more slowly this time, and held out his hand for the horse to sniff. Maverick blew cautiously over Jason's fingers, then allowed him to place his hand on his neck.

"There you go, boy," said Jason, his voice gentle. "It's not so bad, is it?"

After another ten minutes, Maverick began to relax. Amy was glad that she'd spent a good hour with him earlier, working in T-touch circles all the way up his back, shoulders and neck. It would have been even better if she'd had some mimulus flower remedy to soothe his fears, but the massage had definitely helped. He was much more relaxed now, and she could see that Jason was warming up to him.

"He could be a great little horse," he said, and turned to Bill. "Just right. But I'm going to have to see what kind of a ride he is. Any chance of tacking him up? If Ty here can handle him, I reckon I'll be up to it."

"Of course. I'd suggest you try him in the training ring first," said Bill.

"That's fine by me," Jason said easily. "Nothing wrong with having a bit of a warm-up."

While Bill went off to get Maverick's tack, Jason chatted with Amy and Ty, telling them tales of life on the cattle ranch. It was obvious the ranch meant everything to him. "I spent a couple of years working in a bar down in New Orleans," he explained. "It was a lot of fun, but the ranch always drew me back. It's in the blood. Horses and cattle, they're my life."

Amy thought of Carey and wondered what she would make of Jason's words. Perhaps she would realize that moving away wasn't always a solution. But then she remembered what Carey had said in the forest and guessed what her friend's response would be. *The searching is what counts.* She sighed and smoothed Maverick's mane where a tufty part kept springing up. The fact was that things were changing. Maverick was as good as sold, and Carey wouldn't be here much longer.

Bill returned with the tack, and Ty and Amy helped to keep the mustang quiet while he was saddled up.

"He's all yours, Jason," said Ty when they'd finished. "I'll hold him while you mount."

Jason mounted smoothly, but as soon as Ty let go of the bridle, Maverick poked his nose in the air and scooted backwards with his weight deep in his haunches. Jason shortened the reins and tried to drive him forward, but the mustang only fought harder. He shifted back and raised his nose. Amy saw the sweat spread in dark patches across his coat.

"He needs to ease up and let Maverick relax," Ty muttered to Amy.

But Jason had already figured that out. He loosened the reins and sat quietly, waiting for the little horse to calm down. After a few minutes, Maverick stopped sweating, and Jason took up the reins again. With Ty close by, the mustang walked forward, and they all made their way to the training ring.

Taking things a step at a time, Jason eased Maverick through his paces. Jason was a natural rider, with the loose-limbed ease of someone who has spent all his life in the saddle but never been taught in a school. His style seemed to suit Maverick, and as Amy watched them canter round the ring, she felt glad that the horse might have found a new owner. At the same time, though, her thoughts turned to Carey. She didn't doubt that her friend would agree that Jason looked like the right person to take Maverick. But even that knowledge would not make this any easier for Carey.

Jason rode over to the gate, grinning. "Time to get out on those trails, I reckon," he said. "Which way do I go?"

"I'll need to come with you," said Bill. "Bring him up to the yard while I tack up Wishbone."

Amy and Ty walked alongside Jason and Maverick while Bill strode ahead to get his horse ready.

"You'll need to take it real easy out there," said Ty. "He spooks at just about everything, at first. But Wishbone's a natural leader. He'll be a good influence."

"Ah, he'll be fine now," said Jason confidently, clapping Maverick on the neck.

Amy hoped he was right, but she and Ty exchanged concerned glances. It was true that Wishbone was the ideal companion for a nervous horse – he was the big, steady bay that Bill rode at the head of trail rides. But after being bullied in the past, Maverick would never trust other horses very readily.

Bill soon had Wishbone tacked up and swung himself into the saddle. He rode forward and beckoned to Jason, who nudged Maverick with his heels. The half mustang fell in behind Wishbone as far as the gate, then suddenly seemed to realize that Ty and Amy were no longer with him.

He stopped dead in his tracks and gave an anxious whinny, peering back into the yard.

"Hey, come on, boy," said Jason, urging him forward more firmly.

It was no use. Maverick began to fight again, refusing to move, then crabbing stubbornly sideways. As Jason grew more frustrated, Ty and Amy ran forward. Amy grasped Maverick's bridle, throwing Jason a sympathetic smile.

"He'll probably be OK once he gets going," Ty said. "We'll get you out on to the trails."

Amy led Maverick forward through the gate and along the track towards Bill, murmuring quietly to him. Then she let go of the bridle and allowed Jason to ride him forward on his own. This time Maverick obeyed, and Amy and Ty retreated to the gate. They watched until the two horses had disappeared between the trees, then wandered back to the yard.

"Maverick really isn't all that comfortable yet, is he?" said Amy, biting her lip.

Ty sighed. "He'll probably settle down," he said. "He did yesterday. Jason's not a bad rider. As long as he doesn't ask too much of him, they should be OK."

"Well, I hope so," said Amy. She looked around, feeling slightly at a loss. "I think I'll do some grooming while we wait for them to come back. It'll keep me from worrying."

"Good idea," said Ty. "I'll join you."

* * *

They had just tied up Sandy and Rugged Glen on a fence post when Carey appeared in her work clothes. She looked worried and drawn, and Amy felt a burst of sympathy for her friend. It must be terrible, knowing that Maverick's fate was now out of her hands.

"Hi, Carey," Amy greeted her. "I guess you might not want to hear this, but your dad's still out on the trails with the guy who wants to buy Maverick."

"I know," Carey said. "I got back from town early. I saw them go." She sounded miserable.

Amy touched her arm. "Hey, I'm sorry."

Carey shook her head. "It's not that," she said. "Look —" She broke off and seemed to be listening closely to something. She took a deep breath. "Did you hear that?"

Amy and Ty stared at her, confused. "What?" Amy asked.

Carey pointed towards the mountain. Ty and Amy turned, and Amy saw that the sky had darkened in the last half hour. As she strained her ears, she heard a faint rumble, like a logging truck.

"There's a storm brewing," said Carey. Amy realized the rumble she'd heard was thunder.

She frowned. The clouds were still relatively high, and the darker ones were moving slowly away, in the direction of the mountains to the west. "It doesn't look like a bad one, though," she commented. "The forecast was pretty clear."

Carey shook her head. "It isn't anything major, but that doesn't matter. Maverick is terrified of thunder. Just those rumblings would be enough to scare him, and if there's a thunderclap, he'll be out of control."

"You mean he'll bolt?" Ty asked, stepping forward in concern.

"Bolt. Buck. Panic, basically," Carey replied. She looked beseechingly at Amy and Ty. "I know it sounds like I'm trying to interfere, but this is serious. I have to get to Maverick before that happens. I can't let him hurt himself – or anyone else." Amy had never heard her friend sound so vulnerable.

"Get to him? How?" asked Amy. "You mean ride after them?"

Carey nodded. "I can guess which way Dad has gone. Most of the trails take a couple of hours, and he won't have gone out on those. He'll have taken the valley loop. Would –" She gave them another pleading look. "I was wondering if you'd help me?"

There was another ominous grumble from the sky, and Amy felt a splash of rain on her bare arm. If Carey was right, there wasn't any time to lose. "Of course we will," she said quickly. "Which horses?"

"If Ty takes Rugged Glen and follows them, he might just be able to catch up," said Carey. She looked sheepishly at Ty. "I've seen the way you handle Maverick. You might be able to calm him if you get there before me." She glanced down as she spoke, avoiding Ty's gaze.

Amy stared at Carey, surprised. She knew what a big step this was for her, but now wasn't the time to acknowledge it. "Should I come with you?" she asked.

Carey nodded. "I'll take Sandy. You can ride Albatross. We'll take a short cut that might get us to them more quickly if they're more than halfway around."

She didn't need to say any more. Wordlessly, the three of them hurried to the tack room, grabbed the necessary tack, then ran to the horses. More splashes of rain fell on the dusty yard. Amy buckled Albatross's throat lash as fast as she could, her fingers trembling.

"Ready?" Carey cried, and Amy looked up in astonishment. How had she tacked up so fast? And then she saw that Carey was sitting bareback on the chestnut mare and was already halfway to the gate. Amy hesitated. Should she ride Albatross bareback? She felt a strange thrill at the idea.

"Come on!" Carey called over her shoulder, and Amy made up her mind. Leaving the saddle balanced on the stall's half-door, she swung herself lightly on to the horse's back and nudged him forward to follow Carey.

"Ty!" Carey instructed firmly. "Follow the right-hand track. Take the first left-hand fork and keep bearing left. You should catch up with them!" She sounded confident and in control, and Amy felt relieved by her certainty.

Amy glanced back to see that Ty had almost finished tacking up Rugged Glen.

"See you later!" she called to him. "Good luck!" Then she and Carey were out of the yard and on to the trails, pushing the horses into a canter that soon became a gallop. Amy looked ahead at Carey. Her slender legs seemed to be almost moulded to Sandy's back, and Amy felt a thrill of excitement and fear. It was a strange sensation, feeling the powerful muscles of the paint horse so close to her own skin. She rarely rode bareback nowadays, and she knew that a sudden swerve might easily unseat her.

But as the trail narrowed and Carey pushed forward ever faster, Amy felt as though she was melting into the horse's rhythm. Albatross knew every twist and turn of the forest pathways and never checked his long, even stride. The wind whipped at her face, and Amy realized that she could rely on the paint horse to keep her safe.

They reached the edge of the woods and came out in a meadow that sloped gently away down the mountain. A path led straight across it to re-enter the woods on the other side, and Carey pushed forward again, anxiously looking up at the sky. Amy followed her gaze and saw that the dark clouds had blackened further and were lingering over the horizon. As they entered the shelter of the forest she heard a louder rumble, and then in a flash of lightning she saw horses ahead, higher up among the trees, on a trail that led down to meet their own.

Sandy gave a whinny of recognition, and Amy heard raised voices, calling to each other in alarm. She saw a flash of Wishbone's bay coat and the lighter dun of Maverick's. She steadied Albatross and trotted forward more slowly to catch up with Carey, who had just reached the junction with the higher trail.

The other horses came clearly into view. Amy saw Bill on Wishbone, shouting instructions to Jason, who was struggling to keep Maverick under control. The half mustang had his nose in the air and was shaking his head, his terror made plain by the foam around his bit and the rolling whites of his eyes.

Carey jumped down from Sandy's back and began to run towards Maverick. Amy heard her call to the horse, but her voice was drowned out by a sudden, resonating clap of thunder.

It was too much for Maverick. He threw his head down between his legs and bucked. He repeated the motion, again and again – three catapulting kicks that left Jason sprawling on the forest floor. Free of his burden, Maverick turned blindly down the short-cut trail and galloped off, his reins trailing on the ground beside him.

Chapter Nine

Amy's heart almost stopped, but Carey instantly sprang into action. Remounting Sandy in a single bound, Carey tore back along the path.

"Maverick!" Amy heard Carey cry.

Amy looked around. There was still no sign of Ty. Bill had dismounted and was helping Jason to his feet. To her relief, he seemed none the worse for his fall. Fearing for Carey's safety, Amy turned Albatross and headed in the direction Carey had gone. Another clap of thunder echoed through the air.

The rain pelted down as Amy galloped along the path. Ahead, Maverick was careering along, his reins and stirrups flying, and Carey was urging Sandy on, trying to bring the chestnut horse alongside Maverick. Carey was leaning at such an angle that Amy didn't know how she was managing to stay on – and then she saw her friend grab hold of Maverick's saddle. Amy's stomach lurched. Carey was going to vault from one horse to the other.

No! Amy thought. The move would be too dangerous. She urged Albatross forward faster, until she had almost reached the two other horses. Then she saw what was happening. Carey was merely holding on to Maverick's saddle to slow him down and to let him know she was there. She was leaning forward, her legs gripping Sandy's sides, talking to him, and Amy could see that the mustang was gradually easing up. Amy relaxed immediately. She shouldn't have doubted Carey.

Amy guided Albatross along Maverick's other side and reached for his reins, which dangled low, threatening to trip him. With Carey's reassurance and Amy's pressure on the reins, the exhausted horse slowed to a canter, then a trot, and finally a walk. When all three horses had finally stopped, Carey jumped down from Sandy's back and ran directly to Maverick, her face filled with worry. Maverick's sides were heaving and his eyes were still wild with fear. As Carey flung her arms around his neck and buried her head in his mane, Amy felt a lump rise in her throat. If there had ever been any doubt in her mind about her friend's love for Maverick, all doubt was completely banished now.

Albatross and Sandy were blowing heavily, and Amy gave them a couple of minutes to recover while Carey patted and whispered to Maverick. Then Amy reached for Sandy's reins.

"I'll take the other two horses back to Bill," she told Carey. She guessed her friend wanted to be left alone, and in any case it would be the quickest way to help Maverick calm down.

Carey nodded. "Thanks," she whispered.

Amy rode Albatross slowly down the path on a long rein, with Sandy alongside her.

Suddenly, she saw Ty cantering along the path on Glen, and relief flooded her.

"Amy!" he called, urging Glen forward to meet her. "Are you OK?"

"Yes," she managed. "Have you seen Jason? He's not hurt, is he?"

Ty drew up beside her, shaking his head. "No. He's fine. Where are Carey and Maverick?"

"They're OK. I left them to recover," Amy explained. "Maverick's really worked up. I don't think having other horses around will help – especially since the storm's not over yet."

She looked up through the dripping trees at the leaden sky as another rumble sounded from over the mountain.

"It's passing," said Ty. "The rain's slowing down. You look soaked, though."

Amy suddenly realized that she was freezing cold and her clothes were heavy with dampness. Ty didn't look any drier. His hair was plastered to his face, and his wet T-shirt clung to his shoulders.

"We should get Jason back," Amy said, beginning to shiver. "I hope he's not too shaken to ride. He could take Sandy."

Ty smiled. "I think he's taken a few tumbles in his time," he said. "Bill's already put him on Wishbone."

Just then, Bill appeared around the bend on foot, with Jason and Wishbone beside him.

"Is Carey all right?" Bill asked, his face etched with guilt and worry. Amy's heart went out to him. She knew he must feel the burden of responsibility more than anyone. She nodded, and explained what had happened. "If you want to take the other horses back, I'll wait here with Albatross," she finished.

"I can't let you do that," said Bill. "You're soaking wet – and besides, it's better for Carey to make her way back in her own time. The rest of us should head back now."

Amy didn't argue. Bill mounted Sandy and led them along

the short cut, back out over the meadow and through the woods. Amy expected to see Carey and Maverick along the way, but there was no sign of them.

Jason's breeziness had gone, though he was clearly determined to seem unperturbed by his fall. He wanted to know how Carey had tracked Maverick down.

"That was spooky," he said. "Showing up bareback like that. I mean, how did you guys know that he'd choose exactly that moment to turn bucking bronco?"

Amy smiled. "I didn't know," she said. "It was Carey who knew there'd be a problem. She understands Maverick so well. She knew the storm would get to him."

"OK. So why wasn't she around earlier, if you don't mind me asking?"

Jason's voice was curious, and there was an awkward silence.

"She doesn't want to sell him, maybe?" Jason mused at last, drawing his own conclusions. "Well, he's a great little goer, but I'm not sure about him now. Seems to me that – what's her name again? Carey? Seems to me like Carey's the one to take him in hand, not me."

"Carey's leaving," Bill said quietly. "That's why we're selling him. I'm very sorry about all this, Jason."

"Hey, no problem," said Jason. "I've had much worse falls, and I can't say you didn't warn me. Thing is, though –" he hesitated – "I'm kind of superstitious. If I get thrown by a horse the first time I ride him, I reckon it doesn't bode too well, if you know what I mean."

It was a telling remark, and Amy threw him a sideways

glance. Jason's expression was genuine enough, but she guessed that his pride had been hurt in the fall, even if the rest of him hadn't been.

"Well, like I said, I'm sorry," said Bill as the Ten Beeches gateway came into view. "But, to be honest, I can't say I blame you."

Amy and Ty said their goodbyes to Jason, then gave the horses a quick rubdown before going indoors for hot showers. They met back in the kitchen, where Barbara had heated up some beef and vegetable soup. As she served it to them by the wood-burning stove, Bill came in and went off to the bathroom to have a shower, but there was still no sign of Carey. Amy gulped down the delicious soup, eager to get back outside. Surely her friend would have returned by now.

When Barbara left the kitchen, Amy rose to her feet. "I'm going to find Carey," she said to Ty. "Do you want to come?"

Ty shook his head. "I think you should talk to her alone. I'll stay here for a while and dry out by the fire." He smiled. "I'll be here if you need me."

"OK, thanks," said Amy, giving him a smile. "See you later."

She headed outside. The storm had passed, and the air was fresh and tangy with the scent of rain and pine needles. To her relief, she found Carey safely back in Maverick's stall, vigorously rubbing the mustang with a straw wisp.

"Hey," said Amy softly over the half-door. "How's it going?"

Carey looked up. "He's still pretty freaked out," she said. "But he's calmer than he was."

"Have you given him some Rescue Remedy?" asked Amy.

"Some what?" Carey looked puzzled.

Amy explained about Bach flower remedies, and how Rescue Remedy was a combination of flower extracts that was particularly good for trauma and shock. "I have a bottle with me. I'll go and get it," she said. "What about you? You must be freezing. Want me to bring you a sweater and some soup?"

"That'd be perfect," said Carey. "Thanks, Amy."

As Amy ran back to the cabin, it occurred to her that Carey seemed so much more at ease now that she was working with Maverick again. She was back in her element. And seeing her like that made it clear what a sacrifice it was going to be for Carey to leave Maverick behind.

She grabbed a thick fleece and the Rescue Remedy from her room, and poured a mug of soup in the kitchen. Outside, she found the yard suddenly full of horses and trail riders – the afternoon ride had returned. They, too, had got caught in the storm, and the riders were comparing the state of their drenched clothes, laughing.

Amy dodged around them and headed back to Maverick's stall, where she fished the little brown bottle out of her pocket and shook a few drops on to the palm of her hand. Carey watched curiously as she held it out for Maverick to lick.

"I'm surprised Huten didn't use flower remedies," said Amy.

"We have herbal remedies," said Carey. "The same ones used by our ancestors. I bet they work in a similar way."

Maverick licked the drops from Amy's hand, then stood

quietly, nosing at Carey's warm fleece. Carey fondled his ears and kissed the top of his head.

"I've got myself into a mess because of you," she said in a low voice. "A really big mess." She looked across the horse's back at Amy. "Haven't I?" she asked.

It was a difficult question to answer. Amy stroked Maverick's neck, thinking of all the things she had tried to understand about her friend. "I think I'm beginning to see," she said, choosing her words carefully. "This isn't just about Maverick, is it? It's about Huten. I think maybe it's him that you can't let go."

Carey played with the straw wisp, weaving stray pieces back into the main braid. "I feel like I've let him down," she blurted out. "He always expected me to be so strong and unselfish – just like him. Instead, I feel like I keep wanting everything that I just can't have. I want to leave, but I still want Maverick to be my special horse. I keep thinking things over, but I can't seem to see a way out. It's like a jigsaw puzzle, where none of the pieces fit."

Amy nodded. "I get what you mean," she said.

Carey looked at her. "Do you? Do you really?"

"I think so," Amy said uncertainly. "Huten taught you how to gain a horse's trust, and you've done that with Maverick. You value his trust more than anything because it represents all the things that Huten showed you." She paused and took a deep breath. "But if you're really going to do what Huten believed in, you have to let Maverick trust other people and let him go. That's hard because it feels like saying goodbye to Huten as well. It's like you lose both of them at the same time."

Dusk was approaching, and in the fading light Amy saw a tear glistening on her friend's cheek. She waited for a moment while Carey composed herself. Carey wiped her face with her sleeve and cleared her throat. "That's it," she said. "You've got it, pretty much."

Amy smiled. "The thing I don't understand," she went on cautiously, "is *why* you have to go. If you stayed, you could keep Maverick, and you could continue Huten's work. You'll always have the memory of what he taught you."

An image of her mother came briefly into Amy's mind as she spoke. Marion's spirit lived on through the work that she and Ty did at Heartland.

Carey slowly shook her head. "It's no good," she said, her voice breaking. "I've thought about it so much. I have to go. There's nothing more to learn here now that Huten's gone. When he got sick, he told me he knew I'd need to leave Ten Beeches. He gave me his blessing and said it was OK. I couldn't see it at the time – I didn't want to. All I wanted was for him to get better. But he was right."

Amy felt her chest tighten as she remembered Huten's calm, patient wisdom.

"Maybe one day I'll come back," Carey went on. "But not until I've found the things I'm looking for. There's a whole world out there, Amy. I just have to go and find it."

There was a note of anguish in Carey's voice. It was so difficult, feeling close to someone else's pain, and Amy had to swallow down the tears gathering at the back of her throat. "So what about Maverick?" she managed to ask.

Carey's tears began to flow more freely. "Remember what I told you in the forest? Just because you love a place or a person, it doesn't mean you can't leave them. Huten used to say that to me. He knew how restless I was, deep down. So I keep saying it to myself. I hope that if I say it often enough, I'll be able to do it more easily."

She paused, wiping her tears away. When she spoke again, her voice was stronger. "I've been struggling to let Maverick go. I didn't want him to trust anyone else like he trusts me. But after today, I can see it's just not fair to him. He needs to develop confidence with other people, because life's too frightening for him otherwise."

She stroked the half mustang's neck for a moment, then reached for a brisk brush and started brushing the mud from his fetlocks. Maverick snorted, before stretching his head down to nose her hair.

"He's already looking perkier," Amy commented. "The Rescue Remedy's kicking in."

Carey met her gaze briefly. "I'll have to get some," she agreed. "It's obviously good stuff." She moved on to Maverick's hind legs and set to work with the brush again.

Amy watched her for a moment. "So, what are you going to do?" she asked softly.

Carey finished off with Maverick's fetlocks and straightened up. "What Huten would have done in the first place," she replied with a small smile. "I'll train him properly before I leave, so that Dad can trust him with other people."

Amy gave her a quizzical look. "Even trail riders?"

Carey shrugged and grinned. "I think so. I hate the thought of selling him, so I just have to accept that life at Ten Beeches has changed."

"That's wonderful, Carey," Amy said warmly. She hesitated, then added, "You know, Ty and I can help you with that, before we go. Maverick trusts Ty already, a bit. We can build on that."

Carey's face hardened for an instant, and Amy wondered if she'd said the right thing. Her friend had made a brave decision, but that wasn't going to make it an easy one to carry through — especially as she'd hardly taken to Ty in the first place.

But then Carey took a deep breath and nodded. "Well, I've got to start somewhere," she said. "Thanks, Amy. Let's give it a try."

Chapter Ten

"He goes well on the lunge," Amy commented as Maverick trotted round Carey in the training ring. "Do you think he'd do that well for me?"

"I guess we'll have to try it and see," said Carey. She brought Maverick to a halt, then handed Amy the lunging line and whip. "It's not the same as riding him, and in any case, I'll still be standing here. He should be OK."

Amy took Carey's place, making a triangle with the lunging line in her left hand and the whip in her right. With a little flick of the whip, she asked the half mustang to trot again and was delighted when he set off round the ring with his neck arched and his hooves thudding rhythmically on the sand.

It was the next morning. Ty stood with Aiden at ringside, watching while Amy and Carey warmed up the horse. Amy had explained Carey's decision to Ty, and all three of them had eaten breakfast together before starting work with Maverick. The storm clouds of the day before had completely disappeared, and the sun was high in the sky when they led the horse down to the ring, waving to the line of trail riders who were heading into the woods.

"That'll be enough, won't it?" said Amy when Maverick had circled the ring a few times. "We don't want to tire him out."

She brought him to a halt, then gathered in the line and

handed it back to Carey. Aiden headed back to the yard as Ty walked over.

"What next?" Carey asked, stroking Maverick's nose.

Ty and Amy exchanged glances. "Well," Ty began, "I guess you've joined up with him before?"

Carey nodded. "It was one of the techniques that Huten used."

"Of course. Well, it might be a good idea if Amy joins up with him," said Ty. "Or if I do."

"I think it should be Ty," Amy offered. "There's already a bond between them, and that's what we need to work on."

Carey's face became still. She looked down at the line in her hands, and Amy could see how hard this moment was for her – she still desperately wanted to keep her bond with Maverick to herself. She twisted the lunge line around her fingers and said nothing.

"Maybe it's too soon," said Ty awkwardly. "Sorry. I—"

"No," Carey said suddenly, looking up. "It's fine. I'm the one who should be sorry. You're right, Ty, let's try joining up with Mav. I'll go to the gate and watch." She handed Ty the lunge line and walked away, her head bent so that her dark hair covered her face.

Amy met Ty's gaze and smiled. "Good luck," she whispered. "I'll go stand with Carey."

Once Amy and Carey were out of the way, Ty unclipped the line and waved his arms, driving Maverick away from him. The horse gave a snort of alarm and trotted to the edge of the ring, then turned and stared, his nostrils flaring. Ty drew himself up to his full height and drove the horse on again, not allowing him to rest and acting as an aggressive herd leader might do in the wild. This time, Maverick bucked and cantered off, rolling his eyes so that the whites showed.

As Maverick careered round the ring, he spotted Carey watching by the gate. His ears pricked forward and he gave a shrill whinny, then cantered over to her, clearly relieved to see her.

Amy held her breath. If Carey responded now, it would completely undermine what Ty was trying to achieve. But she knew seeing Maverick so distraught would tear her friend apart. The horse seemed to be calling to Carey, begging her to rescue him!

But Carey didn't. Instead, she moved away from the fence and turned her back to Maverick, then walked down the track towards the pasture. Maverick stood stock-still, staring after her. He seemed unable to believe that she had left him and gave another whinny of distress. Amy looked at Carey's hunched shoulders and walked after her, leaving Ty to continue with the join-up process. It was the only way.

Amy caught up with Carey and touched her arm. "Hey. Are you OK?"

Carey looked pale but nodded. "I have to go through with this," she said. "I owe it to Huten – and Maverick."

They reached the pasture gate and leaned on it. Carey cupped her chin in her hands, and they watched a group of the trail horses grazing in the morning sun. To Amy, it seemed like this was the moment when Carey was finally letting go – and following in her grandfather's footsteps more than ever before.

"You know, it may not be much of a consolation, but you'll always be special to Maverick," Amy said. "He'll bond with other people, sure. But the bond with you will always be the strongest."

"I guess," said Carey. "I just hope he'll forgive me. It was so hard, turning away from him – like I was betraying him all over again."

"You haven't," Amy said firmly. "You really haven't. You're just giving him the chance to get to know someone else. Of course he'll forgive you. Horses don't bear grudges like that."

Carey smiled. "You're right, Amy. You know, I wouldn't be able to do this if you weren't here."

Amy felt her cheeks redden in surprise. "Of course you would," she said.

"No, I mean it," Carey insisted. "I knew you'd help, one way or another, like you did last time. That's why I asked you to come."

"Actually, I wasn't sure why you'd asked me at first," Amy admitted. "When you told me you were going to leave, I wondered if you wanted me to persuade you not to, all over again."

Carey shook her head. "I guess it's more that I needed help seeing it through," she said. "You're a good friend, Amy. You help me to get to the bottom of things." She pulled away from the gate. "Let's see how Ty's doing."

They walked back up the track together. As the training ring came into view, they stopped. After being kept in the lonely place at the outside of the ring, the little half mustang now wanted the safety of Ty's company. Amy saw that the horse was giving all the right signals – flicking his ear towards the centre, lowering his head and making a chewing motion with his mouth. These were the signs that horses used to communicate with one another, signs that said, "*I want to be friends.*"

Amy and Carey walked forward quietly as Ty relaxed his aggressive stance and turned his back on Maverick. The horse stopped and stared at Ty, momentarily puzzled. Then he made his decision. Looking more purposeful, he walked over with his ears pricked and nuzzled Ty's shoulder.

Amy felt flooded by warmth and joy. No matter how many times she saw it happen, join-up always seemed like a miracle. It was the basis of all the work she did at Heartland, and she gained as much from it as the horses did. She glanced sideways at Carey. Her eyes were shining with just the hint of tears. Amy was glad to see that, in spite of everything, her friend was moved, too. They stepped up to the gate and entered the training ring.

Ty looked at them and smiled. He walked a few circles round the ring with Maverick following right behind him, as though he couldn't get close enough. Then Ty made his way over to Amy and Carey. As he did so, Maverick spotted Carey and whinnied in greeting. He stopped. For a moment, he seemed uncertain what to do – stay close to Ty or break away and go to Carey. But then, as Carey ran towards him, he snorted and trotted over to meet her.

Carey threw her arms around Maverick's neck. "Hey, Mav,"

she said. "You were a star." She blinked back her tears and buried her face in the horse's mane.

Maverick butted Carey affectionately. Carey beamed, and Amy could only begin to guess how relieved she was that Maverick still chose to be with her.

"Not much of a contest here, Carey," said Ty with a grin. "You're still Maverick's favourite!"

For once, the whole family sat down to breakfast together the next morning. Barbara had got up early to bake fresh honey and walnut muffins, which she brought out of the oven and put straight on the table. They smelled delicious.

"I hope you two like barbecue," she said to Ty and Amy. "We thought we'd have a few friends over this evening, since it's your last day. We'll have a meal in the backyard. How does that sound?"

"Fantastic," said Amy and Ty in unison, reaching for the muffins.

"Good," said Bill. "I'm pretty busy today — Aiden's taking out a group on an all-day ride, so I might need help chopping up some wood, if anyone's handy with an axe."

"No problem," said Ty. "I think it's Amy's turn to work with Maverick, so I could make myself useful doing something else." He glanced at Amy and Carey. "Is that a good plan?"

Amy looked at Carey, then nodded. "Thanks, Ty. Maybe we can come and gather up the logs when we're done," she said.

After eating as many of the muffins as they could, Amy and Carey headed outside. Aiden was just mounting Sandy, while three trail riders sat waiting for him by the gate on Brandy, Mushroom and Ruby. Amy and Carey waved them off, then went to Maverick's stall. The little mustang was dozing but shook his mane and whickered as they opened the door.

"You know, I think he's happier already," said Carey as she led him into the yard. "You're a relative stranger, but he seems to accept you almost completely."

"I guess I've spent a lot of time with him this week," said Amy. "He's had a chance to get used to me."

"That's been the problem with Dad," said Carey with a sigh. "He just doesn't have much time, so Maverick has never really relaxed around him. It's going to be tricky finding people to work with him once you leave."

"Aiden would help you, wouldn't he?" suggested Amy. "He was watching us work with him yesterday. And I bet there would be plenty of trail riders who'd spend some time with him, even if you didn't want to let them ride him right away."

Carey grinned. "You have an answer for everything," she said. "So, what's our plan for today?"

They agreed that Amy should pick up from the work that Ty had done and join up with Maverick.

"I'll keep my distance today," said Carey as they led Maverick to the training ring. "He'll respond more quickly if there aren't any distractions."

Amy nodded, feeling slightly nervous. It was very rare for join-up not to work and, as Carey had pointed out, Maverick was getting used to her already. There was no reason why he shouldn't respond to her, just as he had to Ty. But somehow she felt there was a lot hanging on it. Joining up with Maverick felt like a special gift from Carey – she was sharing Ty and Amy with the horse she loved most in the world, and Amy didn't want anything to go wrong.

But there was no need to worry. Maverick was a fast learner, and as Amy drove him away from her round the training ring, he showed much less anxiety than he had the day before. She kept him cantering around for a few laps without letting him slow down or rest, and he quickly came to a decision. He would much rather be with Amy in the centre of the ring than alone on the outskirts.

When Amy saw the signs she was looking for, she turned away and waited for Maverick to come to her. She soon heard his soft footfalls behind her on the sand and felt his warm breath on her neck.

"Hello, Maverick," she murmured happily, stroking his nose.

While she was waiting for Carey to come back, Amy wandered round the ring, enjoying the bond that the mustang had forged with her. Now that he had chosen her company, he didn't want to let her go. No matter which way she turned or how fast she walked, he kept close behind her, his muzzle almost touching her shoulder. He seemed like a different horse from the stubborn, frightened creature that she and Ty had coaxed to the pasture on their first day at the house.

Amy waved as Carey appeared at the gate. To her surprise, Carey's arms were full of tack, and Amy jogged over to the gate.

"Looks like it went well," commented Carey, seeing that

Maverick had followed right behind. She smiled. "I thought you might like to take it a step further. How about riding him?"

Amy grinned and instinctively squeezed her friend's arm. "That would be great," she said. She searched Carey's face. "If you're really sure."

For a split second, Carey hesitated. Then she nodded. "There's no one I'd rather share him with," she said. "Come on. Let's tack him up."

Within minutes, Amy was astride the little mustang. She stroked his neck soothingly before asking him to move around the ring.

"He responds well to voice aids," Carey told her, walking alongside. "I trained him that way. It makes me feel closer to a horse than just using hands and legs."

Amy nodded and smiled. "OK. I'll try it. Trot," she said clearly, giving Maverick a squeeze with her legs. He was surprisingly responsive and broke into a springy trot. After a few circuits, Amy pushed him into a canter, grinning as she passed Carey at the ringside.

"He's great!" Amy called, and did one more round before turning him towards the gate.

"I have a suggestion," said Carey when Amy came to a halt. "It's your last day. How about we take Maverick on to the trails?"

Amy was dubious. "Do you think he's ready?" she asked. "I don't want to upset him."

"He'll be fine. And I'll be there," said Carey. "He's going well for you now. I'll ride Albatross, and Ty can ride Glen again if he wants."

Amy's face split into a smile. "You mean you want Ty to come with us?"

Carey looked at her steadily. "He's been part of this, too," she said. "A big part. Come on, let's rescue him from his logs. There's something I want to show you both."

The trail that Carey had chosen rose steeply up the mountain, more steeply than any of the paths that Amy had ridden so far. At first, Maverick was nervous around Glen and Albatross, and even kicked at the grey gelding when he came up too close behind him.

"I'll keep my distance," said Ty from behind. "I guess he needs time to relax."

Amy nodded and rode on, talking quietly to the mustang and keeping up a firm but gentle pressure with her legs. Reassured, Maverick began to walk more steadily, following Albatross up the winding path. Up, up they climbed, the horses blowing with the effort and the sun beating down strongly as the tree cover became thinner.

After climbing for almost an hour, they emerged from the forest on to a rocky track that led round the side of the mountain. Here, there were shrubs and bushes growing among the rocks and, to her delight, Amy spotted a groundhog crouching on a boulder. The squat brown-furred animal regarded her for a few moments, its cheeks working as it munched a mouthful of leaves, before it turned tail and vanished behind the rock. Amy wondered if her companions had seen the creature, too, but they both seemed lost in thought.

Carey led them onward along the track, which levelled out so that they could trot. They rounded a corner, and Amy suddenly saw what they had come for. Ahead of them stretched a breathtaking panorama. As far as the eye could see, there were rolling, forested mountains, glistening here and there where streams formed silvery ribbons on the landscape.

Carey brought Albatross to a halt, and Amy nudged Maverick alongside them. "Wow," Amy whispered. "This is really something."

As Ty caught up to them, he pointed ahead. "Is that a bald eagle?" he asked.

There was a dark speck wheeling in the sky, and as it drew closer Amy could see its massive outspread wings and striking white head.

Carey nodded. "I often see them up here," she said. "That groundhog had better watch out."

"So you did see him!" Amy exclaimed with a laugh. "Carey, thank you for bringing us here," she added softly, still gazing ahead. "It's amazing."

The horses turned their faces into the breeze and stood quietly as the three riders soaked up the view. There was no sound, apart from the shrill, mewling call of the eagle.

Then Carey spoke, her voice serious. "Whenever I doubt my decision to leave Ten Beeches, this is where I come," she said. "Here, I can *see* that there's a whole world out there. I'm not making it up. It's real. It stretches out as far as your imagination will take you, and beyond."

"You sound like Huten," Amy said softly. "That's just the sort of thing he would have said."

"Well, guess what?" said Carey in a lighter tone, turning Albatross back on to the path. "He's the one who showed me this spot. Surprised?"

"No," Amy said with a smile. "I think Huten saw further than any of us ever will."

Chapter Eleven

For the rest of the day, Bill and Barbara kept everyone working hard. Ty and Amy tacked up five horses for Bill's afternoon trail ride, then finished chopping logs for the fire. Carey went indoors to help Barbara prepare the food. Later on, when both Bill and Aiden had returned, Amy watched Bill construct a simple spit on the lawn behind the cabin, so that the chickens could be suspended over the fire.

"I'll have to rotate the chickens by hand," he explained, showing her how the skewer rested on two supports. "You can help me keep an eye on them, if you like. We need to keep turning them so that they're nicely cooked and crispy all over."

"Sure," said Amy. "When do we light the fire?"

"Now," said Bill. "I'm just about to start it up. Want to help?"

As Carey and Barbara brought out bowls of salad, fresh corn on the cob and crusty bread, darkness fell and the flames from the fire shot brightly into the sky. Guests began to arrive and gathered around the blaze. They were mostly people from the town – friends and relatives of Bill and Barbara's, and one or two younger people as well. When the flames died down a little, Bill skewered the marinated chickens and set them to cook on the spit, then made a barbecue grill at the edge of the fire and placed the cobs of corn on it. Before long, the tantalizing smell of roasting chicken and corn began to fill the air.

Amy and Ty wandered among the guests with Carey, who

introduced them. Everyone was very friendly and curious to hear about Heartland. Amy felt as though they were guests of honour, and her heart swelled with happiness and pride – here she was with Ty, away from home, representing Heartland's work to a group of strangers. Leaving Ty chatting with Carey, she went back to the fire and turned the chickens. Aiden came to help her.

"I enjoyed watching you guys yesterday," he commented. "Maverick's always been a one-woman horse, but he was doing well with you all."

Amy smiled. "I noticed you watching," she replied. "I mentioned to Carey that you might like to work with him, too."

Aiden raised his eyebrows. "I'm not sure she'd be up for that," he said.

"Try her," said Amy. She looked across at her friend, talking with Ty on the other side of the fire. "I think you'll find she is."

"Well, I guess I'll need to get to know the little fella if he's going to stay," said Aiden thoughtfully. "Thanks, Amy. I'll give it a try."

At last the food was ready, and Bill cut the chickens into portions. Amy thought it was one of the most delicious meals she had ever eaten – the chicken and corn both infused with the delicate scent of pinewood smoke, with Barbara's tangy fruit punch to wash the food down. She ate cross-legged on the grass between Carey and Ty, watching as Bill threw more logs on the fire to build up a blaze once more.

Gradually, everyone settled around the fire. Someone produced a guitar, and Bill began to sing. It was an old local melody, and most of the guests joined in, clapping along and providing various harmonies. More songs followed, and a friend of Barbara's recited a lighthearted poem about a groundhog and a bullfrog having an argument. Amy hugged her knees to her chest, full of contentment and peace.

Then Carey raised her hand. Amy glanced over at her friend, who looked calm and serious. Silence fell, and everyone stared into the crackling fire as she started to speak.

"There was once a horse that lost its master," Carey began. Her voice took on a soft, pleasant cadence that was wonderful to listen to. "One day he was there, and next he was gone. The horse looked all around the place they lived but found no sign of him. It was a mystery, and the horse was deeply grieved.

"So the horse began to look further afield. He galloped over the plains and through the forests, asking after his beloved master.

"'We haven't seen him,' said the beavers. 'We are too busy building our dam.'

"The horse thanked them and went on. He met other creatures, but none of them had seen his master. The eagles flew too high, and the salmon swam too deep. The bobcats and the big black bears thought only of what they could hunt. No one had any news to offer. So the horse thanked them all and went on.

"On and on he went, through summer sun and bitter winter winds and snow. He grew hungry and thirsty and very weary, searching for the master he loved so much. At last he knew that there was nowhere else to look. He had seen the whole world."

129

Carey paused and looked around at the mesmerized faces. Amy watched a twig catch fire and twist into a glowing red ember. She thought of Albatross, the faithful, willing horse who must have missed Huten so much.

"And so he went home," Carey went on. "He lay down and closed his eyes. There was no strength left in him, and slowly, surely, he felt his life ebbing away. And then, through the growing darkness, he heard a voice – an old, familiar voice, the one he knew so well.

"'If you had seen me, you would have stopped,' whispered his master. 'Because I was not there, you kept going. You have seen all there is to see and learned all there is to learn. You have done well, my faithful friend. Some things are better seen alone. I am with you now. Sleep in peace.'"

Carey's voice trailed off, and Amy felt tears pricking her eyes. A ripple of applause went around the fire, and she joined in, blinking the tears away. Bill threw another log on to the fire, creating a shower of sparks, and Barbara bustled inside to make hot cocoa.

Another story began, and the group settled down to listen. But next to her, Amy felt Carey move away. She looked around and saw her friend disappearing into the shadows.

"Back in a minute," she muttered to Ty, squeezing his arm. "I'm just going to check on Carey."

Ty nodded, and Amy got to her feet. A few feet away from the fire, she was engulfed by the darkness and had to wait a few moments for her eyes to adjust. Then, up ahead, she saw the shadowy figure of Carey wandering under the beech trees behind the cabin. As Amy watched, her friend leaned against one of them, then slid her back down the trunk so that she was sitting on the grass, looking up at the stars, with her arms wrapped around her knees and a blade of grass twirling in her fingers.

Amy approached quietly, but Carey heard her footsteps. She turned her head and smiled as Amy squatted down next to her. They sat in companionable silence for a few moments. Then, by the light of the moon, Amy saw the sadness on Carey's face.

"Was that an old story?" Amy asked.

Carey nodded. "Huten used to tell it." She leaned her head on the beech trunk. "What do you think it means?"

Amy pictured Albatross once more as she thought of the horse in the story – an image of patience, tolerance and endurance. She remembered how calm Albatross had seemed earlier. But it was not only Albatross who came to mind. There was Carey, too, and her determination to search for experience, whatever the cost.

"I guess it means you should be faithful to the things you believe in," Amy said after a moment. "However difficult it is, or wherever it takes you."

Carey nodded. "Yes. I think you're right," she said. "And more than that, there's something about answers never being where you expect to find them." She turned to Amy and smiled wryly. "Look at Maverick. I never thought that the answer for him would lie partly in Ty."

Amy raised her eyebrows. "What do you mean?"

Carey studied her hands and frowned. "I guess I owe you

both an apology," she said. "I was pretty mean to him when you first arrived. I think I wanted your visit to be just like last time – when Huten was still here. Just you and me riding off into the forest and doing stuff together. Somehow I thought we could recreate it all."

"I know what you mean," said Amy. "I felt the same way when Ty first suggested coming along. It was just so special, last time. I was afraid we wouldn't get to really talk to each other with someone else around."

Carey looked surprised. "I had no idea you felt that way, too," she said. She hesitated. "I thought that with you being so close to him, you wouldn't want to be close to me as well."

"Of course I do!" Amy exclaimed warmly. "In fact, I sort of resented him coming at first. But now I'm glad he did. We couldn't have brought back the past, no matter how hard we tried."

"No," agreed Carey. "Things change, don't they? We all move on to new things. New beginnings."

"And you've made a new friend in Ty," Amy pointed out.

Carey looked at Amy, her expression questioning. "Do you think so?"

Amy smiled. "I'm sure of it."

"Well, I'm really grateful for all the work Ty's done with Maverick. I'd like him to know that."

"I think he already does," Amy promised. "He's better at understanding what people are feeling than I am."

Carey laughed softly. "I find that hard to believe," she said. "You've always managed to get a read on me."

Amy wanted to tell her friend how much her words meant, but she could only smile at Carey, her heart brimming with happiness. She leaned back against the tree trunk with her friend to gaze at the stars. They sat there in silence, and as Amy felt the night breeze on her face, she closed her eyes and smiled. She knew now, with a deep, warming certainty, that this trip was every bit as special as the last one.

Chapter Twelve

When Amy woke the next morning, she lay quietly for a few moments, listening to the beech trees outside move in the wind. Her visit had come to an end all too soon. She didn't want to leave this beautiful place.

But then she shook herself and jumped out of bed, thinking of everything that lay ahead – seeing everyone back at Heartland, hearing about Lou's latest wedding plans, and finding out how all the horses were doing. She thought of Spindleberry and smiled. She would be so glad to see him! But she didn't feel as anxious as she might have a week ago. She knew Joni would have had done a good job with the young horse.

Ty wanted to get an early start on the road, so after a quick breakfast, he and Amy packed and began to say their goodbyes. Bill kissed Amy's cheek and shook hands with Ty, while Barbara loaded them with sandwiches for the trip. Then she hugged them both and stood next to Bill to wave them off.

Carey came forward and hesitantly gave Ty a hug. "Thanks so much for everything," Amy heard her say.

Ty hugged her back. "Anytime," he said quietly.

Then Carey turned to Amy and reached for her hand. "I'll stay in touch," she said, her dark eyes smiling. "I promise."

"You'd better!" Amy replied, swallowing a lump in her throat. "We can't neglect each other this time." She wanted to thank Carey for all she had taught her, but there was too much to say. Instead, she hugged her friend tightly, then turned and clambered into the pickup next to Ty.

"Bye!" everyone chorused as Ty started the engine. "Come back soon!"

It seemed that much longer than a week had passed since they had driven up the Ten Beeches driveway. Both Ty and Amy lapsed into silence as the pickup bumped down on to the highway. Steadily, the mountains turned into hills and the landscape became more familiar. Amy thought that Ty seemed rather quiet. "Are you OK?" she asked.

Ty smiled. "Just thinking," he said. "I'm so glad I came with you on this trip. There's no way to get a sense of a place like that unless you go there yourself."

"My thoughts exactly. I'm glad you came, too," Amy said warmly. She looked out the window, thinking, then turned back to Ty. "I would never have guessed what was going on with Carey and Maverick – or that you'd end up being so involved. You helped them both so much."

"Well, it turned out a lot better than I thought it would," Ty joked. "Anyway, I think I gained more than I gave."

Amy nodded, letting the week's events wash over her, remembering certain vivid images – riding Albatross through the forest, her moment with Ty by the stream, the soaring bald eagle, Carey's story by the fire and, best of all, joining up with Maverick.

As the familiar Heartland driveway and the white weatherboarded farmhouse came into view at last, Amy's heart gave a bound. Lou and Grandpa hurried out to meet them, smiling and waving. After lots of hugs and greetings, Lou ushered them inside. Amy was dying to look around the stables first, but Lou had food prepared. "I hope you're hungry," her sister said. "Nancy and I have been trying out lots of recipes. We've saved a big batch for you."

Amy laughed, thinking of the mound of sandwiches they'd eaten along the way. "We'll try to fit in a morsel or two," she said, smiling at Ty. "I take it the wedding plans are going well?"

Lou nodded, pushing open the kitchen door. "Nancy's been fantastic," she said. "We've got it all worked out. It'll be delicious."

Judging by the wonderful smells that greeted them, Amy could tell it was true. She and Ty sat down at the table and began to tell Grandpa about their time at Ocanumba while Lou made tea and served them thick slices of apple pie. They were starting to nibble at the pie when Joni popped her head in the door.

"Hi there! I saw Ty's pickup," she greeted them. "Did you have a good time?" She joined them at the table and accepted a slice of the pie from Lou. "I've been eating so many experiments this week," she said, "I'm surprised I haven't turned into a guinea pig."

Amy grinned and asked about the horses. "I hope you've been managing OK."

"Oh, it's all been fine," Joni assured her. "Lou and Jack helped with the chores, and Ben came over a couple of times. I've had time to do some work with the rescue horses. In fact, I don't know whether Lou mentioned this –" She cast a glance at Lou, who shook her head. "Well, Sasha's owner spotted Bear when she came by to pick up Sasha. She's interested in him as a beginner's pony for her daughter."

"That's great!" exclaimed Amy. "It'll be an ideal home for him. Has anyone said yes?"

"Not yet," said Lou. "We thought we'd wait until you got back."

"So what about the others?" Amy knew there was one horse she wanted to know about more than all the others, but she forced herself to wait.

"Well, Sasha turned out just fine. Her owner was really pleased with her. Libby's not progressing any faster, but she'll get there," said Joni. She pushed away her empty plate and sighed. "That was scrumptious. Thanks, Lou."

Finally, Amy could wait no longer. "What about Spindleberry?" she asked.

Joni smiled at her. "I knew you'd be curious about him," she said. "I love working with him, Amy. He learns so fast! He's becoming a perfect gentleman around the stables – very well behaved. You'll be proud of him."

Amy tried to smile. Of course she was pleased that her yearling was doing so well, but couldn't he have missed her just a *little* bit? Then she was seized by guilt.

Hadn't she learned anything from seeing Carey let go of Maverick? A wave of sympathy swept over her as she realized just how hard it must have been for her friend.

Then another thought crossed her mind. *Carey is leaving Ten Beeches*, she said to herself. *That means she has to share Maverick. But I'm still here. I don't have to share Spindle – not yet.*

Slightly horrified at herself, she pushed the thought away. This wasn't just about her happiness. It was about Spindle's, too. Huten had been right all along, giving Albatross the gift of generosity. Good, noble Albatross had room in his heart for everyone, even when his master had gone. And that was the way it should be.

Amy suddenly knew she couldn't wait any longer – she had to get out and see Spindle. She gripped Ty's hand under the table. "Do you feel like taking a walk around the yard?" she asked. "I think I need to stretch my legs."

Ty nodded. "Good idea," he said, taking a last forkful of pastry. "Thanks for the pie, Lou. It was fantastic!"

Ty and Amy handed Lou their plates, then headed outside. "Let's go down to the pastures," said Amy. "I guess most of the horses will have been turned out for the afternoon."

As they wandered down the track, Amy peered eagerly over the fences, looking for the little roan with slender legs. *Please let him remember me*, she thought. They leaned over the gate to the most distant pasture, and one by one the horses raised their heads to look at them.

"Spindle!" Amy called.

The yearling was on the far side of the field cropping the grass with short, busy snatches. He lifted his head at the sound of Amy's voice and stood still for a moment, his whole body alert. Then, with an excited whinny, he leaped forward and cantered to the gate.

Amy laughed out loud and let herself into the paddock. Spindleberry rushed up to her, and she flung her arms around his neck. She looked at Ty, delighted.

"I don't think he's forgotten you!" said Ty, laughing with her.

As Spindle nuzzled her shoulder, Amy reflected once again on the past week. There was so much to be gained from letting go. Sharing Spindle with Joni for a few days made their reunion now all the sweeter.

The Heartland routine re-established itself quickly. Sasha's owner came to pick up Bear, the first of the five rescued horses to move on to a new home. Her thirteen-year-old daughter was thrilled with her new horse; she hadn't been riding long, but Amy was confident she'd make a kind, undemanding owner for the good-natured gelding. Two new horses arrived for treatment, and Amy's days were packed with work. Her summer vacation was racing by, and she dreaded the thought of going back to school for her final year. Splitting the duties of Heartland and school was always stressful.

Then, when she was sweeping the yard one morning, Lou's voice called from the house. "Amy! A letter just came for you!"

Amy propped the broom against the tack room door and jogged indoors. Lou handed her the letter, and she stared curiously at it. The handwriting was bold and sloping. She didn't recognize it, and the postmark was illegible. Hastily, she tore it open and began to read:

Dear Amy,
How's it going? As promised, I'm staying in touch. We don't have
e-mail access at the house, so here's an old-fashioned letter. I hope

139

you and Ty are doing fine at Heartland. I really want to come and see you guys one of these days. Thanks so much for dragging yourselves all the way here — you have no idea how much it meant to me. (Thank Ty for me, will you?)

I just got some great news, so I thought I'd let you know. I was offered a job at a camp as a counsellor. It sounds like a lot of fun, and you know how much I like working with kids. They have programmes all year round, but I'll get time off to travel and go back to Ocanumba for breaks. I'll be getting training, though at my interview they said that my storytelling and work with trail riders give me a good head start.

Maverick's doing just great now. My dad and Aiden took time to help me work with him, and Aiden has been able to take him out on the trails with a few of the more experienced riders. I start work in a month, and I think he'll be fine by then. Mom and Dad are really happy. I guess they felt bad about selling him, even though they knew they had to.

So that's my news, Amy. Thanks again for being such a good friend. Your coming here changed everything, for the best. Write when you have a chance.

Lots of love,

Carey

Amy read the letter several times before folding it and putting it in her pocket. She smiled to herself and went to find Ty.

Ty was straightening out the feed room and making a list of herbal remedies that were running low. Amy stood in the doorway, and he looked over at her.

"Everything OK?" he asked.

Amy fished in her pocket and handed him the letter, going into the tack room and sitting on a stool while he read it.

He scanned it quickly, then looked up. "That's so nice of her, to say all those things. Sometimes it's easier to put things in writing," he said. "So, it looks like she's going after all. It won't be easy, leaving her family and all those memories behind."

"No," agreed Amy. She looked thoughtfully at Ty. "But she knows that Huten's blessing goes with her. She can hold on to that, whatever new places she discovers." Amy paused, remembering something. "There was this thing that she kept saying to me while we were there. Something that Huten taught her. It was so powerful."

She hesitated. Carey's words echoed her mind, and she realized she had never said them out loud.

Ty waited expectantly. "Go on," he prompted.

Amy took a deep breath. "She said, 'Just because you love a place or a person doesn't mean you can't leave them.' I thought it was pretty scary to think like that. But I guess she really believes it. And now she's acting on it. She knows there are other things she needs to do."

A silence fell between them for a moment. Then Ty handed Amy the letter. "That takes courage," he said softly.

Amy reached out for the letter, holding on to his fingers briefly as she took it from him. Their eyes met.

"Yes," she said, with a little smile. "I guess it does."

141